FIGHTING BACK HARD

Slocum's right hand snapped across his body and whipped the Colt from the holster; he thumbed the hammer back as he drew, let it slip as the muzzle swung into line. . . . The man with the shotgun twisted in the saddle as Slocum's slug took him with a heavy thump. Both barrels of the shotgun discharged, the thunderous roar almost atop the blast of Slocum's pistol. Buckshot whistled past Slocum's hat. . . .

JAKE LOGAN

HELLTOWN TRAIL

B

BERKLEY BOOKS, NEW YORK

HELLTOWN TRAIL

A Berkley Book / published by arrangement with
the author

PRINTING HISTORY
Berkley edition / January 1993

ISBN: 0-425-13579-9

A BERKLEY BOOK ® TM 757,375
Berkley Books are published by The Berkley Publishing Group,
200 Madison Avenue, New York, New York 10016.
The name "BERKLEY" and the "B" logo
are trademarks belonging to Berkley Publishing Corporation.

PRINTED IN THE UNITED STATES OF AMERICA

10 9 8 7 6 5 4 3 2 1

1

Scott's Ford had aged since Slocum's last visit.

The town had outgrown its wide-open, hell-raising ado-
lescence of a few years ago, when the trail herds came to
the railhead from Texas. The rails had pushed west, and the
drovers followed the iron ribbons that stretched across the
Kansas prairie. Now, Scott's Ford had settled into a comfortable adulthood.

Slocum leaned against a porch rail of the Exchange Hotel
and surveyed the community's main street. There was little
traffic along the wide thoroughfare. In the trail drive days
cowboys, cattle buyers, gamblers, merchants, and teamsters
would have been jockeying for space, even on a Sunday evening. Now the stores were closed in observance of the sabbath;
most of the townsfolk on the street today were headed home
from evening worship at the small but serene whitewashed
church at the end of the business district.

Slocum decided he liked Scott's Ford better as a raw and
untamed bronc than as a gentle buggy mare.

What he missed most was Aunt Sophie's Social Club across
the tracks from the Exchange Hotel. The elegant former whorehouse was now a respectable general store. Slocum was more
than a bit disappointed at that. *Progress,* he groused inwardly,
can be inconvenient as hell at times.

He had been looking forward to doing business again with

the little brunette called Katie. She had been one of Slocum's all-time favorites. Katie had the greatest legs Slocum had ever seen, and she was damned good at her work. He wondered what had happened to her after Aunt Sophie's had started selling cooking pots and flour instead of prime women. *Probably moved on to another railhead town,* he thought, *or maybe even married and settled down.* Whatever the case, Slocum wished her luck.

He pulled a cigarillo from his shirt pocket, fired it with a sulphur match, and drew the rich smoke deep into his lungs. He pinched the head of the match and broke the wooden stem before tossing it aside, a habit born of riding the tall grass country, where a single spark from a lucifer or a cigarette could trigger a prairie fire that could wipe out two counties. He squinted through the blue-gray smoke toward one of the few buildings that showed some sign of life. At least the town still had one saloon. The wait until morning wouldn't be a total loss after all.

Slocum tried to shake away his disappointment over the loss of Aunt Sophie's. It had been a good trip anyway, he reminded himself. He'd had no trouble trailing the half dozen saddle horses to the Rafter C, a day's ride northwest of town. The Rafter C's owner was a good judge of horseflesh and didn't believe in horse-trading bullshit any more than Slocum did. He looked the mounts over, agreed that the price was fair, and closed the deal by writing out a bank draft for three hundred dollars and pouring a couple of shots of fine Kentucky bourbon. Slocum's own horses, the leggy sorrel saddle horse and the stocky bay that served dual roles under pack and saddle, were tended and quartered in the Scott's Ford livery. Slocum had moved his equipment and himself into a comfortable room at the Exchange, soaked away the trail grime in his first real bath in days, and filled his belly at the hotel's downstairs restaurant. *A couple of drinks to cut the last of the trail dust,* Slocum thought, *and this mother's child will feel human again; at least it'll be something to pass the time.*

When the bank opened for business the next morning, he would exchange the bank draft for cash and be on his way.

He tugged his hat down more firmly against a gust of wind from the Kansas plains and strode toward a two-story building and its weathered Trail's End Saloon sign. Slocum stepped aside and touched his fingers to his hat brim in greeting as a shiny black surrey trimmed in gold paint whispered past on freshly greased wheels. The attractive, middle-aged woman on the front seat smiled pleasantly in return. The man holding the reins nodded curtly, more in annoyance than greeting, Slocum thought. The driver wore an expensive black silk suit, a silver belly hat, and the expression of a man with a constant bellyache. A strikingly pretty girl, a younger version of the older woman, ignored Slocum completely and stared straight ahead from the backseat of the rig. She wore a flowing green dress that contrasted nicely with her shoulder-length strawberry blond hair. The dress covered her from throat to high-top button shoes, but it didn't conceal the blossoming woman's figure underneath. Her lips were drawn into a thin line, and there was an aloof, cold look about her. Slocum idly wondered what she would be like if she smiled. Or did she ever smile?

He dismissed the brief encounter from his mind and pushed open the door of the Trail's End.

The drinking establishment was like many Slocum had frequented in his travels. A pine bar stretched most of the length of the room, its top scratched and stained. A few cowboys leaned against the bar, whiskey glasses or beer mugs before them. At the tables scattered about the saloon, a couple of poker games were in progress. The games didn't seem to be high-stakes affairs; the players were laughing and joking, and men didn't do that when there was big money on the table.

At one end of the bar a worn staircase, its rails polished smooth by the traffic of many hands, led to the second floor. Slocum's spirits picked up a bit. Unless Scott's Ford was completely dead and embalmed, a saloon with an upstairs meant there were women available somewhere. The thought reminded Slocum it had been a long time since he had last shared a woman's bed. Too long.

A smoke-stained mirror, cracked at one corner, hung above the backbar where a variety of bottles were on display. The bartender was a bear of a man, with a full beard and mustache, thick forearms covered with dense hair, and a patch of fur that bristled at the opening of his checked shirt. The barkeep greeted Slocum with a nod.

"What'll you have, friend?" the hairy one asked.

Slocum nodded toward the backbar. "Bottle of Old Overholt and a glass should do the job."

The barkeep chuckled. "It'll do, all right. Put hair on a man's chest tonight and fuzz on his tongue in the morning." He brought the bottle and a glass. The bottle was still sealed, which meant the liquor hadn't been watered down, and the glass was clean and polished. Slocum raised his opinion of Scott's Ford a notch. "Two dollars," the barkeep said.

Slocum fished a pair of silver dollars from his pocket and placed them on the bar. They disappeared under a big, hairy hand. "If you need something else, friend, just holler. Name's Doc." The furry one turned away to refill glasses and mugs along the bar.

Slocum poured two fingers of whiskey into the glass, sipped the liquor, and sighed in contentment. It was the real thing— smooth, uncut, went down easy, and lit a small but comfortable fire in his stomach.

Slocum had the feeling he was being watched. It wasn't an unusual sensation. He was accustomed to being noticed, though he had never learned to like it. At just over six foot one, lean, with jet black hair, green eyes, and a Colt Peacemaker revolver slung crossdraw style on his left hip, Slocum knew he stood out in most crowds.

He turned to again survey the crowd. Most of those who met Slocum's gaze quickly glanced away. Three men at a table near the far end of the bar stared at him with more than a little interest. Two of the men appeared to be cowhands, their stubbled faces darkened by sun and wind around thick, untrimmed mustaches. The third seemed little more than a boy. He wore the range garb of the working cowboy, but it was obvious the clothes hadn't been off the store shelf very long. His unlined face was framed by sandy hair under a wide-brimmed Stetson pushed back on his head. The youth's skin seemed a bit flushed. The young man dropped his gaze and leaned forward as one of his older companions muttered something, then looked up to stare again at Slocum.

Slocum fought back a twinge of irritation and tried to ignore the kid and his two drinking buddies. Trouble was the last thing on Slocum's schedule for the day. He tossed back the whiskey in the glass, refilled it, and motioned to the bartender.

"Doc, have you been around town long?" Slocum asked.

The big man shrugged. "Three, four years."

"Maybe you can tell me whatever became of a woman by the name of—"

"Slocum!" The call, in a familiar alto voice, brought Slocum's head around and a wide grin to his lips. Katie stood at the top of the stairs, a hip cocked against the railing and a smile flashing white against her dark skin.

"Never mind, Doc," Slocum said over his shoulder. "I just found her."

He barely had time to turn around before Katie scurried down the stairs, dashed across the floor, and threw herself into his arms. She squeezed him hard, a genuine hug of affection. "Slocum, you long-legged son of a bitch," she muttered against his chest, "I ought to whop you alongside the head with a trace chain, leaving a girl alone for all these years."

Slocum returned her embrace, his heart light in his chest. "God, Katie, it's good to see you again." He pushed her to arm's length. "You haven't changed a bit, girl," he said. It wasn't exactly true, Slocum knew, but it was close enough. Katie was a bit thicker in the waist and slightly broader astern than Slocum remembered, but she still had that pixie face with its upturned nose that wrinkled when she grinned, the brown hair still cut short and in ringlets even though it now showed touches of gray. And she was still one hell of a fine-looking woman. Her hazel eyes sparkled with that glint of mischief Slocum had come to know so well.

"You, sir, are both a fibber and a cad of the first order— and I thank you for the compliment even if it isn't true. What the hell have you been up to, you saddle tramp?"

Slocum shrugged. "Staying alive, Katie. And thinking of you often."

Katie laughed, the sound a throaty slide down a musical

scale. "Like hell you have. I'll bet there are little green-eyed kids scattered from Canada to Mexico by now."

Slocum became aware of the silence that had fallen over the saloon. He knew everyone in the place was watching them, but he didn't give a damn. He pulled her back to his side. "How've you been, Katie?"

"Sort of—" She paused, then chuckled. "I was about to say up and down, but I suppose you know that."

Slocum motioned to Doc for another glass and poured Katie a stiff drink. He became aware of something else starting to go stiff. The smell of her alone was enough; add in the memories that still seemed fresh in his mind, and it made a combination that quickened his heartbeat. He watched as Katie lifted the glass and knocked the shot back without wincing. Katie could handle whiskey better than a man twice her size—which wouldn't be all that big. Slocum refilled her glass.

"When I rode in and saw Sophie's place closed, I was afraid you'd moved on, Katie," Slocum said, his tone sincere. "The low point of my day, that was."

Katie pressed closer to Slocum, a firm hip snug against his body. She wore a pale yellow dress, cut low; Slocum saw the quickening rise and fall of her upper breasts. "I've got a lot more to say to you, saddle tramp," she said, her voice husky, "but I'd rather not do it here for all the world to see. I've got a room upstairs if you're interested."

Slocum flashed a grin at her. "Any time I'm not interested in you, Katie, just go ahead and call the undertaker, because I won't be breathing. Lead the way, girl, and don't get side-tracked for any better offers."

Slocum swept the bottle from the bar. Katie downed her second drink, picked up the two glasses, slipped her free hand beneath his arm, and winked up at him. "I've never had a better offer, Slocum."

Katie's room was bigger and better furnished than her room at Sophie's had been. An oversized four-poster bed draped in a deep-blue velvet spread dominated the center of the room. Along one wall stood a clothes rack, a bureau, and a cedar chest; at the side of the bed a sturdy table held a water pitcher, a porcelain bowl, and neatly folded towels. It was the opposite wall that drew Slocum's attention. It boasted a polished mirror the length of the bed and four feet high.

"Katie, girl," Slocum said as he motioned toward the mirror, "you're getting downright decadent."

Katie grinned at him over her shoulder as she poured whiskey into the two glasses and placed them on the table at the bedside. "Us older women have to learn new tricks to keep up with the young ones, Slocum," she said. She turned and came into his arms. She kissed him deeply, her tongue flicking against his own, her pelvis thrust tight against him. Slocum felt the swelling grow in his Levi's. He ran his hand down her back to the round flesh of her buttocks. They were as muscled and firm as he remembered.

After a moment Katie pushed away. She was breathing heavily. "Dammit, Slocum, we're wasting time," she said. She reached for the buttons on her gown. "Get your clothes off, cowboy. You can't do either of us much good that way."

Slocum undressed as he watched Katie strip. That in itself was damn near worth the price, he thought. The gown slipped to the floor. Katie wore nothing underneath. Slocum's breath caught in his throat; this was one of the sexiest women he had ever met, and that covered a lot of the country. Katie's breasts weren't large, but they were perfectly shaped and still firm, the nipples erect in the center of a circle of dark pigment the size of a half dollar. And she still had the finest legs Slocum had ever seen, smoothly muscled with full thighs and calves and trim ankles. And at the junction of belly and thighs lay a thick triangular patch of hair so dark it appeared to be black.

Slocum stripped off the last of his clothing and knelt to pick up Katie's gown, intending to drape it over the clothes rack.

"Don't bother, Slocum," she said, her voice almost hoarse. She stripped the cover from the bed, climbed onto the center of the fresh white sheets, and lay with her legs spread in invitation.

"My God, Katie," Slocum said, almost awestruck, "I had forgotten how—"

"Shut up, cowboy, and come here," she interrupted.

Slocum went.

He lay beside her for a moment, his hands stroking the

smooth skin of her breasts and ribs, then drifting down to caress the dense tuft of dark, wiry hair at her crotch. Katie moaned softly. She reached down. The warmth of her fingers cradling his taut scrotum triggered a new fire in Slocum's groin. Her hand closed around his swollen shaft. She used it as a handle to pull him onto her. Katie's breathing was rapid; Slocum could feel the pound of her heart against his chest. She spread her legs further and guided him into her.

Slocum lay still for a few seconds, savoring her snug, moist heat. Then he moved his hips, withdrew almost completely, before slowly sliding back into her. Katie arched her back, her hips rising to draw him in, and a whimper sounded from the back of her throat. Slocum felt the first droplets of sweat bead where their skin met. He repeated the slow, gentle stroke, then began to pick up the pace in response to Katie's growing urgency beneath him. Moments later, her breath caught in her throat as she buried her face against Slocum's shoulder and drove her pelvis against him. She cried out as her muscles suddenly convulsed; Slocum felt the contractions deep inside her. The sensation pushed him to the point of no return. The first explosion into the hot, wet depths brought an intensity of pleasure that bordered on pain. Katie's fingers dug into Slocum's back as his first release gave way to a series of deep, jerking pulsations. The throbs continued for what seemed an eternity before Slocum finally lay spent and gasping for breath, filmed with the sweat that drenched both their skins. His breathing gradually returned to normal as his heartbeat slowed. After a few moments he felt himself go limp inside her. He became aware that he was resting too much of his weight on her body and lifted himself with an effort onto his elbows. He looked into her eyes and saw the mist of tears there.

"Damn, Slocum," Katie said, her breath still coming in small gasps, "you're good. With you, I never have to fake it."

Slocum shifted his weight and traced a finger tenderly along her jawline. He knew she was telling the truth. He had been with the bored ones who didn't even try to enjoy it; he had been with the ones who tried to make him believe they enjoyed it; and he had been with a few, like Katie, who damn well did enjoy it—and it wasn't that hard to tell the difference. It was the difference between a whore and a woman.

"You're something special yourself, Katie," Slocum said. "Which reminds me. I forgot to ask how much I owe you."

Katie chuckled. "This one was—you should pardon the expression—on me, Slocum. Christ, the way I feel right now, I should pay you."

Slocum shook his head. "Everybody has to eat, girl. Whatever it is, it was worth every dime." A sudden thought struck Slocum. "Katie, how much do you normally make in a night?"

Katie lifted her shoulder in a half shrug. "Maybe fifteen, twenty dollars." She grinned. "I've started limiting my clientele, you might say. I'm not as young and active as I used to be."

"I'm going to make you a proposition, Katie."

Katie's nose wrinkled in the familiar grin. "That's my business, Slocum. Propositions."

Slocum rolled off Katie, lay on his side, and cradled her head beneath his arm. "I'd give twenty dollars not to have to share you with anybody else tonight." He let his free hand drop to her breast. "That was too quick. I don't think I'm caught up yet."

Katie sighed, a wistful look in her eye. "Me, either, Slocum. But honestly, you don't have to pay. I'm yours for free. Any time you're in town."

Slocum snorted in mock disgust. "Don't argue with me, woman. I'm bigger than you are. I've got a room at the Exchange. Why not spend the night with me? You wouldn't be bothered by any of your regular customers that way."

Katie leveled a lecherous wink at Slocum. "You've got yourself a deal, cowboy," she said. She sat up, frowned, and slipped a hand to her crotch. "God, Slocum, you made one hell of a mess down there."

"I think I had some help," Slocum replied with a wry smile. He rolled off the bed onto his feet. His knees felt like the joints had been disconnected. "I'll tell Doc you're booked up for the night. Feel up to staggering over to the hotel?"

"I'll meet you there later. I need to freshen up a bit first and gather a few of my things." She nodded toward the bottle on the table beside the bed. "You might pick up another jug for us, Slocum. We may need it before the night's over."

Slocum reached for his Levi's. "I'll do that." He fished in a pocket, found a gold double eagle and the key to his room at the Exchange, and handed them to Katie. "The key's in case you get there before I do. It's room five, at the end of the hall to the left." He leaned over and kissed her tenderly. "I'll go square things with Doc."

Slocum finished dressing, made his way downstairs to the bar, and waved to get the bartender's attention.

"Doc, I'll need another bottle of Old Overholt," Slocum said, "and if anybody should ask for Katie, tell them she's not available tonight."

Doc nodded and glanced along the rows of bottles on the backbar. "I'll fetch a new bottle from the back. The ones I've got out here have all been opened."

Slocum leaned against the bar and waited patiently as the bartender headed for a storeroom. He became aware of being watched and glanced in the backbar mirror. The young man in the new clothes pushed his chair back and rose, unsteady on his feet. Slocum wasn't sure if it was the whiskey or the high heels of new boots that made the youngster wobbly. He obviously wasn't accustomed to either. The sandy-haired kid stopped fifteen feet from Slocum.

"So you're Slocum." The youth's voice was slurred and his strange amber-colored eyes seemed a bit out of focus.

Slocum nodded. "I'm Slocum. Something I can do for you?"

"I hear you're a real stud hoss of a pistolero," the young man said.

Slocum shrugged and fought back a surge of irritation. "Some say that."

The youth leaned forward on the balls of his feet, his right hand near the butt of a pistol tied down impossibly low on his thigh. The holster and gun belt were as new as the clothes and the kid, Slocum noted. The youngster jabbed his left thumb over his shoulder.

"My friends Shorty and Pete over there say I'm faster than you are, Slocum." The voice was clipped, the words tinged by a northern or eastern accent.

"You might be, son," Slocum said, trying to control his growing anger. "Tonight, I'm in no mood to find out. I've got no quarrel with you, except that maybe you pick the wrong friends. Besides, one or the other of us will live a lot longer if we just let it drop. I'll buy you a drink."

A couple of cowboys leaning against the bar glanced at Slocum and the kid, then stepped back, leaving beer mugs behind. At the table beyond, Shorty and Pete scrambled aside, toppling a chair in the process. They had enough sense to get out of the line of fire if it came to a fight, Slocum realized.

"The hell you say, Slocum," the kid said. "I'm calling you out. You afraid of me?"

Slocum pinned a hard glare on the unlined face. He saw no fear in the amber eyes, only the glazed reflection of too much whiskey. "Son, I'm a little cautious about anybody carrying a gun. Might be a good philosophy for you to think on some, too."

"You're not scaring me, Slocum," the kid said. "Now, reach for that pistol."

The damn fool isn't going to back off, Slocum thought. *But maybe there's a way I won't have to kill him.*

At the corner of his vision Slocum saw the bartender emerge from the back room, bottle in hand. Doc took a quick glance at the two men, then quietly placed the bottle on a shelf, reached beneath the bar, and brought out a sawed-off double-barreled shotgun. "I don't want any trouble in here, gents," Doc said.

Slocum sighed. "I'm afraid it's gone too far, Doc. The kid here won't let it drop. I won't shoot up the place, just put a couple in his gut. Keep an eye on his two drinking buddies over there for me."

Doc nodded. Slocum quit worrying about the kid's friends. The bores of that shotgun would look like stovepipes to them.

"All right, son," Slocum said. "If you've just got to have a fight, I've no choice but to give you one." He raised a hand. "But let's study out something first. You know, it takes guts and a little luck, along with a quick draw, to be a gunfighter. You feel up to a little test?"

Confusion muddled the amber eyes. "What are you talking about, Slocum?"

"I think you've got guts. Let's find out how stiff your back-bone really is." He held out his hand. "Give me your gun."

The confusion swirled deeper in the youth's eyes. He slipped the pistol from its holster and handed it to Slocum.

Just what I thought, Slocum mused, *this kid's dumb as a stump and green as last year's cheese.*

Slocum hefted the kid's handgun. It was a single action Army Colt .45 with a seven-inch barrel and smooth mahogany grips. Slocum tilted the barrel up, flipped open the loading port, and worked the ejector rod. The gun was so new the action was still stiff and untuned. Six cartridges fell into his palm, one at a time.

"What the hell are you doing?"

"Hang on a minute." Slocum dropped five of the cartridges onto the bar. He palmed the sixth, tapped the cartridge rim against the receiver as if chambering the round, clicked the loading port shut, and spun the cylinder. He slipped the sixth cartridge into his pocket. "Five out, one in," he said. "Now I'll do the same to my side arm."

Slocum eased his Colt .44-40 from the crossdraw holster and ejected all five cartridges. He put them on the bar next to the kid's .45 ammunition. He clicked the cylinder shut and spun it.

"Now, son," Slocum said as he leaned forward, dropped the youth's Colt back into the new holster, and sheathed his own weapon, "we'll see how your luck—and mine—runs tonight. Each gun has one cartridge. We draw and pull the trigger. If a live shell turns up under the hammer, the winner walks away. The loser won't be doing much of anything." Slocum grinned at the kid. "If neither gun goes off, we can tell by the click of the hammer who won the contest," he said. "If it works out that way, you call the winner. I trust you be honest."

Indecision and the first hint of fear flickered in the boy's amber eyes.

"Tell you what," Slocum said, "just to make it a little more interesting, let's bet on it. Say ten dollars?"

The young man swallowed hard, then nodded.

Slocum stood relaxed. He let his gaze go cold and hard as he stared at the kid. "Any time you're ready, son," he said.

The kid's fingers twitched above the walnut grips. Then he made his move.

Slocum waited until the youth's .45 had started to move from the holster. Then he slapped his hand against the butt of the .44, flexed his knees, drew, and eared back the hammer all in one smooth motion. The dull click of the hammer on Slocum's pistol sounded before the kid had his weapon completely clear of leather.

"Bang," Slocum said.

The boy's eyes seemed as big as silver dollars as he stared at the bore of Slocum's handgun lined on the second button of his shirt. He stood, frozen with surprise and fear, for an instant. Then, with fingers beginning to tremble, he dropped his Colt back into the holster. His shoulders slumped.

"Jesus," the kid said, his voice little more than a quavering whisper, "I never saw anything that fast."

Slocum picked up the cartridges from the bar and began reloading his weapon. "You owe me ten bucks, young man. I'd say you got off cheap for the lessons."

"Lessons?" The boy's face had gone chalk-white. He was sobering up mighty fast, Slocum thought.

"Gunfight lessons," Slocum said. "Lesson one: *Never* hand your gun to a man you're going to try to kill. That, my friend, was the dumbest damn thing I've ever seen." Slocum thumbed the final cartridge home and clicked the loading gate shut. "Lesson two: Know your liquor limits. Too much whiskey slows the reflexes. Lesson three: Pick your friends a little more carefully; they damn near got you killed. Lesson four: Never call a man out in a gunfight. There's always somebody faster and somebody who shoots straighter. There are other lessons here. I think you can figure them out for yourself."

Slocum pushed the .45 cartridges down the bar to the kid. "Better reload. Can't tell when you might need the cartridges."

The dazed youngster finally tore his gaze from Slocum's face. He picked up the brass and started fumbling cartridges into the weapon. His fingers trembled. He rotated the cylinder, then looked up. "There's only five cartridges here."

"Oh, I almost forgot," Slocum said with a slight grin. He dug into his pocket and brought out the sixth .45 cartridge. "Unless you know you're going into a fight, always carry the hammer over an empty chamber. Drop a Peacemaker with a cartridge under the hammer and it might go off. Forty-five slug can tear a man's balls right off. At your age I don't think you're ready to part with them just yet."

Slocum tossed the sixth cartridge to the amber-eyed youth.

"You mean my gun was empty?" Disbelief widened the boy's eyes. "You tricked me, Slocum."

"Guess I did," Slocum said with a shrug. "My gun was empty, too. Nobody gets killed in a gunfight with an empty weapon."

A touch of color returned to the boy's face. It was the first flush of embarrassment and humiliation. "Slocum, you could have killed me." He dropped his gaze to the saloon floor.

"No doubt about it. You've got a lot to learn." Slocum waved a hand in dismissal. "Don't try me again, son." A hard edge crept into his tone. "I might not be in such a mellow mood next time." He glared for a moment toward the youth's two companions. "How about you two? You seemed almighty hot for a gunfight. Want to try me? This time there'll be live ammunition in the gun."

The two men glanced at Slocum, at the big-bore shotgun in Doc's hands, and at the young man standing by the bar. Their faces paled. They spread their hands with care well away from their weapons and shook their heads. "We didn't mean nothin', Slocum," one of them said. "We was just funnin' a little."

"That kind of funnin' can get a man seriously dead," Slocum said, his tone icy. He turned away from the two men. "If you'll hand me that bottle, Doc, I'll be moving along." He held his hand out, palm up, and wiggled his fingers. "Kid, pay up. You owe me ten dollars."

The youth fumbled in his shirt pocket, brought out a gold coin, and dropped it into Slocum's hand. "You may be dumb as dirt, son, but at least you pay off your bets. See you around, if you live long enough."

Slocum took the bottle, left Doc a dollar tip from the change, turned his back on the boy and his two companions, and strode toward the door. He heard the excited chatter start in the saloon as the crowd began to rehash the confrontation. Slocum stepped into the street, drew in a breath of the cool evening air, and grinned in satisfaction. It was shaping up to be a fine night, he thought as he walked toward the Exchange Hotel.

2

Scott's Ford was fully awake by the time Slocum and Katie had finished breakfast at the downstairs café in the hotel.

Slocum could tell from the expression on Katie's face that she was tired but content. It had been a somewhat intense night without a lot of sleep, but it was worth it, he reminded himself. He hadn't felt so loose and relaxed in months.

He waved off the waitress's offer of a refill on the coffee, pushed his chair back, and stood. "The bank will be open for business in a few minutes, Katie," Slocum said. "You might as well go back upstairs and get some rest."

Katie grinned at him, a twinkle in her eyes. "No way, Slocum," she said, "I'm not letting you out of my sight until you ride out of this one-horse town. Besides, it's time I did a little banking myself. Maybe the walk will do me some good. I've got a few stiff and sore spots this morning."

Slocum chuckled. "You're not alone in that, girl," he said. "I would welcome your company. Anytime."

The smile faded from Katie's face. "Not many men would care to be seen in public with a whore, Slocum." Her voice was soft, her tone sincere. "You'll never know how much that means to me." The impish grin returned. "Not to mention the fact that I'll be the secret envy of all the fine, upstanding ladies of the town today."

She let him pull the chair back for her and assist her to

her feet. "Sometimes you show flashes of being a gentleman, Slocum. If you ever decide to settle down—" her voice trailed away, the invitation unfinished.

Slocum grinned at her. "I'll remember that, Katie. You can bet on it."

Outside, she slipped her arm around his waist and squeezed him briefly. The quick embrace pushed against the hideout gun Slocum had tucked into an inside belt holster at the small of his back as he dressed. The weapon was a .38 Colt sheriff's model with a bird's head grip and the barrel cut off to three inches. It wasn't pretty or especially powerful, but it would do the job at close range. Slocum made a habit of carrying a backup gun when he would be toting cash around. Scott's Ford seemed tame enough, but a man never knew when somebody might try to lift his poke. Three hundred dollars would be a hell of a temptation to some men. Even if he didn't need it, the short-barreled pistol was a comfort to Slocum.

Traffic was picking up on the town's main street. Buggies, surreys, and ranch wagons jockeyed for space among pedestrians and saddle horses along the broad stretch of roadway. Slocum guided Katie across the busy street.

The Scott's Ford Bank & Trust building was one of the older structures in town, but it was sturdy, even down to the polished mahogany bench along one wall. Barred plate glass windows at the front combined with the glow of lanterns to illuminate the interior. An elderly teller sat in a barred cage. He wore a green eyeshade and sleeve garters, with wire-rimmed spectacles perched near the end of his nose.

Slocum and Katie were the bank's first customers of the day. She led him toward the teller, who glanced up at the sound of her footsteps. His smile of greeting deepened wrinkles in a face that showed the stamp of wind and weather despite its owner's having an inside job away from the elements.

"Good morning, Miss Katie," the teller said. He had a deep, resonant voice and brown eyes that twinkled as he peered over the spectacles.

"Morning, Mr. Curry," Katie said. "How's the family?"

Curry chuckled in genuine amusement. "The wife's mean as ever, but the grandkids are doing great. They take after me, I reckon. What can I do for you today?"

Katie propped her small leather handbag on the ledge before the barred cage and pulled out a slightly frayed coin pouch. "A deposit today, Mr. Curry," she said, handing over a stack of coins. "I think there's seventy dollars there."

The clerk counted the coins with quick, practiced efficiency, scribbled an entry in a ledger, and made a notation on a slip of paper. "Your receipt, Miss Katie. Something else I can do for you?"

Katie nodded toward Slocum. "This is a friend of mine. He has a bank draft he would like to convert to cash."

Slocum plucked the draft from his shirt pocket and handed it to the clerk. Curry studied the draft for a moment, then nodded. "Sure. I don't see any problem, but we will need to get Mr. Tucker's approval on a sum of this size." He disappeared from the cage and a moment later walked through a swinging gate into the main bank lobby. "If you'll follow me, please, Mr. Slocum?"

"I'll wait for you out here, Slocum," Katie said.

Slocum nodded and followed the clerk toward a heavy oak door at the rear of the bank. Near the door, behind its own protective barred cage, stood one of the most massive safes Slocum had ever seen. *Not even a Pennsylvania coal miner could hack that thing open,* Slocum thought. He stepped into the bank owner's office and felt his brows lift in surprise.

The man behind the mahogany desk was the driver of the surrey Slocum had stepped aside for the day before. And seated at the banker's right was the strawberry blond girl. She still wore the solemn, almost pinched expression he had seen in the back of the surrey. *If she would only smile,* Slocum thought, *she would be a real beauty.*

"Mr. Tucker, this is Mr. Slocum. He has a draft drawn on the Rafter C. The amount is substantial enough to require your approval."

The banker stood and offered a hand. "Will Tucker, Mr. Slocum." The banker's grip was warm, but a bit limp; the man still looked like he had a bellyache, Slocum thought as he returned the handshake. Tucker nodded at the young girl. "My daughter, Victoria," he said.

Slocum touched fingertips to his hat brim and nodded a greeting to the young woman. She returned the nod, but her expression remained cold and aloof.

"Victoria is my number-one assistant," the banker said. "You might even call her the vice president of this operation." Slocum detected a not of cautious pride and fondness in the banker's tone. Slocum decided the banker had a right to be proud. If the girl was as bright as she was pretty, she would be a real asset to the bank.

"Well, Mr. Slocum," Tucker said after examining the bank draft, "this seems to be in order. I hope you aren't offended that my teller had to check with me first. We like to make sure the bank drafts we receive are authentic."

Slocum nodded. "No offense taken, Mr. Tucker. That seems to be a good policy."

"Very well, then. If you will accompany Mr. Curry to the cashier's window, he will give you the money—in any denomination or form you like."

Slocum followed as Curry strode back to the cashier's cage. The teller's step was spry and alert, considering his age. A few minutes later Curry counted out the last of the gold coins and pushed them through the opening in the bars to Slocum. "You might want to count them, Mr. Slocum, just to double-check. I don't often make a mistake when it comes to money, but no man is beyond—" Curry's voice suddenly broke off; his eyes went wide as he stared toward the door.

"Nobody move!"

Slocum glanced over his shoulder. The gravelly voice came from behind the twin bores of a shotgun. The hammers were at full cock. The man behind the smoothbore was blocky, trail-soiled, with a bushy, tangled beard. His eyes were cold and hard. A second gunman, with a ragged scar that slashed from forehead to earlobe across an eye clouded and sightless, stood against a wall a few feet from the door, a rifle in his hands.

It was the third man who drew most of Slocum's attention. He was tall, rail-thin, with dirty brown hair that brushed against stooped shoulders. He wore a frayed frock coat, a battered and dusty stovepipe hat, and held a Colt .45 pistol in his right hand. His eyes were a pale, almost colorless, blue. They held the fevered look of a madman. "This is a holdup, my friends, a shearing of the sheep," the thin man said. "The root of all evil is money. It is my calling to remove this cause of woe from this town of sinners!" The voice was reedy but strong, the words spoken in the cadence of a man behind a pulpit.

Slocum calculated his chances. It didn't look good. Against the man with the pistol he might have a chance to draw the Peacemaker at his hip and fire before lead hit him. With luck he could also take the man with the rifle. But against a cocked smoothbore, there was no way.

Bastards, Slocum thought, *why pick today to rob the damn bank?*

"Get those hands in the air," the man with the shotgun said. He pointed the muzzles directly at Slocum. "You there—the one with the pistol on backward. Ease that gun out. Left hand, thumb and little finger. Slow."

Slocum hesitated. He felt Katie's body press against his left side. "For God's sake, Slocum, do what the man says." Slocum heard the raw fear in her voice. "He'll kill us all!"

Slocum lifted the .44-40 from its holster, crouched, and placed the weapon on the floor.

"Kick it over here," the bearded one said.

Slocum shoved the weapon with his boot. It skittered across the floor and bumped against the man's foot. Slocum watched for an opening, a chance to go for the hideout gun at the small of his back. But the man with the shotgun knew what he was doing. He kept the twin bores pointed at Slocum and never lowered his gaze as he stooped, picked up the Colt, and thrust it into his waistband.

"Now step back. Leave that money right where it lays."

Slocum did as he was told, a cold fury building in his gut. He held his anger in check. The money could be recovered or replaced. A life—his or Katie's—couldn't.

"You there—in the cage." The thin man aimed his pistol at the teller's forehead and tossed a burlap sack onto the counter. "Empty that cash drawer into the bag. Sanctify the servant of the Lord, or let him be your death! Move quickly, man!"

Curry blinked in owlish surprise behind his spectacles, momentarily frozen in shock. The thin man cocked the pistol.

The distinctive four clicks of the Colt hammer jolted the teller into motion.

Slocum could only grit his teeth against his growing rage, wait, and listen to the clink of coins—including his own three hundred dollars—as Curry scooped money into the burlap sack. "The paper money, too," the thin man said. Curry complied, then held the bag aloft.

"That's all there is," Curry said. There was no fear, only a cold anger, in the teller's tone.

"Then to greener pastures shall thou move," the thin man said. "To the strongbox, sinner—the haven where the rest of the evil dwells."

"I can't open the safe," Curry said. "I don't have the combination."

Slocum glanced toward the bank president's office as the door creaked open. "What's going on out here?" Tucker demanded as he stepped into room. The girl stood at his side, her gaze darting from one gunman to another. Her face went pale.

"It's a holdup, Mr. Tucker," Curry said. These men—"

The thin man's pistol whipped around to cover the banker and the girl. "You there." He motioned with the gun muzzle. "Come here, child."

Slocum wanted to shout a warning to the girl; with luck, she could maybe make it back inside the office with its thick door and be safe. But it would mean almost certain death for everyone else. He could only watch as Victoria Tucker, her lower lip trembling in fear, stumbled toward the thin man. The tall one stared at her for several heartbeats. "Be ye the virgin of Babylon or the whore of hell?"

"I don't—don't know what you mean," the girl stammered.

"Leave her alone, mister," Tucker pleaded. "Don't hurt her, please."

The tall man reached out, pulled Victoria to him, and twisted an arm behind her back. She whimpered in pain. The frock-coated man put the muzzle of his Colt against her throat. "Open the safe or I'll kill her."

"I'll open it, mister," Tucker said, his face the color of ashes, "just don't hurt my daughter." Tucker hurried to the safe. He fumbled the combination on the first attempt, had to try again, and finally the door swung open. A stack of bills and two bags of coins waited inside the vault. The tall man nodded toward the teller.

"Gather it up, sinner. Bring all the filthy money to me. Quickly, or the girl's blood will stain this temple of money changers."

Curry scurried to the safe. Perspiration painted a sheen on the bald spot in back of his head as he scooped the loose bills into bank bags. Moments later the aging teller carried the bags to the thin man and dropped them at his feet.

"There, mister," Curry said. "That's all there is. Let the girl go."

The washed-out blue eyes glittered. "I think not, friend. I think I will take her along. If anyone tries to stop us or to follow, the girl will die. When we have reached a safe haven, I will release her unharmed."

"Please, mister! For God's sake, let my daughter go," Tucker pleaded. The banker's face was twisted in fear and desperation.

"She rides with us." The thin man let the muzzle of the Colt fall away from Victoria's neck, stooped, and lifted the heavy money bags as if they were weightless. "We will now take our leave of this hellhole of sinners." The thin man paused to glare at the banker. "Remember, friend. We have your daughter. Her fate is in your hands." The outlaw leader backed toward the door, flanked by the man with the shotgun and the scarred one with the rifle.

"Jubal, deliver your message. Remind them of the Lord's wrath against the money changers," the tall man said as he stepped through the doorway.

The rifleman raised his Winchester, a twisted grin on the scarred face. "You move too damn slow, old man," he said. He fired. Over the earsplitting crack of the muzzle blast Slocum heard the slap of slug against bone; the teller's head snapped back. For an instant Curry stood, a small dark hole in his forehead. Then he tumbled backward. At Slocum's side, Katie cried out in horror; he grabbed at her, missed, and she ran toward the downed teller. Slocum's heart skidded as the shotgun swung toward Katie. The smoothbore bellowed as

Slocum slapped his hand to his back, whipped out the .38, thumbed the hammer on the draw, and slapped a shot toward the man with the shotgun. The bearded man grunted and staggered as the slug hit; Slocum fired again, the impact of the lead driving the man back another half step. The second barrel of the shotgun discharged as the outlaw went down. A cloud of buckshot ripped into the floor at Slocum's feet.

Slocum whirled to face the man called Jubal. The Winchester swung toward Slocum as Jubal yanked at the lever to chamber a fresh round. Slocum held the trigger of the .38 back, thumbed the hammer and let it slip as the Colt settled into line. Jubal grunted in shock and surprise as the soft lead slug slammed into his shoulder. He dropped the rifle, crouched, and ran toward the door. Slocum fired again, saw Jubal's body jerk, and then the scarred man was gone.

Slocum swung the pistol barrel toward the bearded man lying on the floor. The shotgunner moaned and stirred. Slocum shot him again—in the back of the head.

Seconds later Slocum heard the clatter of horses' hooves on the street and the excited yells as the town's residents realized what was happening. A half dozen gunshots rattled along the street, then a stunned silence fell over the town.

Slocum knelt beside Katie and blinked against the sting in his eyes. The buckshot charge had struck her high on the back and shattered her right rib cage. Splinters of bone showed through the blood that pulsed over the shredded cloth of her dress.

"Slocum, I—"

"Hush, Katie." Slocum's voice cracked. "Don't try to talk. You're hurt bad."

A small hand reached up and closed on the sleeve of his shirt. "Slocum—I—I'm sorry."

They were Katie's last words. A few seconds later she died in Slocum's arms. Slocum crouched for a moment, cradling the small, shattered body to him. He swallowed hard against the lump in his throat and tried to fight back the sharp pain in his chest. Her blood soaked his shirt. Slocum didn't notice.

Then, slowly, the agony of loss and helplessness gave way to the smoldering embers of renewed rage. Slocum lowered the small form to the floor. "Those bastards will pay for this, Katie." His voice was little more than a whisper. "No matter where they go or how long it takes, they'll pay. I promise you that."

Slocum gradually became aware of the growing crowd inside the bank. The jumble of voices began to take shape.

"What happened?"

"Bank holdup. Three dead in here."

"Get some horses! Get a posse!"

"No!" Will Tucker's shout brought the comments to an abrupt silence. "No posse. They've got Victoria. They'll kill her if anybody tries to follow them." The banker's eyes glittered in pain and shock. His gaze flitted about, unable to settle on any one person or object. He was, Slocum knew, a man close to losing his grip on reality.

Slocum stood and looked down one last time at what had been Katie. "For Christ's sake, will somebody please cover her up!"

A young cowboy standing just inside the doorway hurried to the bloody bundle on the floor, whipped off his linen duster, and draped it over Katie's body. Slocum realized he still had the .38 in his hand. He tucked the weapon back into its belt holster. He went to the downed outlaw, grabbed a shoulder, and heaved the dead man onto his back. Slocum pulled his Colt from beneath the man's waistband and holstered the pistol, then strode to the banker's side. "Any law in this town, Mr. Tucker?"

Tucker blinked his way back to the real world. "Not at the moment. Sheriff's gone to Dodge to deliver a prisoner. We don't have a deputy or even a town marshal."

"You have a telegraph station?"

"In the depot across the tracks."

"Someone take care of Katie," Slocum snapped. "I'm going over there and get the wires hot from here north to Canada and south to Mexico and get a description of those men out. I'm going to see if I can put names to them."

"Victoria—"

"I think she'll be safe—for a time at least—if nobody tries to tree them." Slocum turned to stare at the small, bloody bundle that only moments ago had been a living, loving woman. "In the meantime, we've some people to bury."

Victoria Tucker clung to the cantle of the saddle behind the thin man, reality pushing aside the stark terror that had paralyzed her mind since the holdup.

Images of the holdup flickered through her brain. It seemed she could yet feel the touch of the cold, round muzzle of the pistol against her throat, hear the sounds of the gunshots from inside the bank, feel the rough hands of the tall man in the top hat as he mounted, yanked her up behind him, and drove his spurs into the big bay gelding. Moments later, four more men closed behind them, quirting and spurring their mounts into a dead run, firing wildly over their shoulders as people scattered in the street. At the edge of town, a fifth rider leading two pack horses joined the group.

The cold grip of dazed fear rode with her as the outlaw band thundered down the main road leading west from Scott's Ford, then reined abruptly from the rutted roadway and charged through the tall prairie grass.

In those first few minutes she had been frozen with shock. It was as if she were an observer, standing outside her own body, watching the terrible sequence of events unfold with someone else in her place. Then the detached sensation faded. The thought flashed through her mind to throw herself from the horse's back; a quick glance over her shoulder told her that would mean being killed or maimed beneath the hooves of horses following close on the bay's heels. Her instinct to live was too strong. She settled down to concentrate on hanging on, to keep from falling beneath the horses' hooves. The pound of saddle skirts against her buttocks jarred up her spine, turned her vision fuzzy and jerky. She felt the sting as the skin on the inside of her legs chafed against leather and horsehide.

The headlong race ended three miles from town as the tall man hauled back on the reins. Victoria felt the labored heave of the horse's sides against her legs as the animal tried to pull air into tortured lungs. Dust swirled about her as the other men reined in.

Victoria stared at the horsemen in the half circle facing the tall man in the frock coat. The scarred man with one eye—Jubal, the bandit leader had called him—slumped over the saddle horn, moaning in pain. At his side a stocky, swarthy-faced man with a black stubble of beard held Jubal in the saddle.

"What ails your friend, Clell?" the tall man asked.

"He got shot back there in the bank, Preacher. That tall jasper had a hideout gun. He put a couple holes in Jubal. I think he killed Lloyd."

"How badly is Jubal injured?"

"How the hell should I know?" the man called Clell snapped. "I ain't no doc. I know it don't look good. His shoulder's busted and I think one slug tore up a kidney."

The tall man called Preacher snorted in disgust. "Fools and knaves. A simple mission, yet one of the Lord's soldiers dies and another is wounded by a simple Philistine. Dirk, give Clell a hand. Minister to the halt and lame as best you can and leave the rest to the Lord."

A tall, spare man with smoke-colored eyes, shoulder-length black hair, and angular features that hinted at Indian ancestry dismounted and strode to the injured man's side.

The fourth man was near middle age, stocky, with a head that seemed undersized perched on thick, muscular shoulders. It seemed to Victoria that he had no neck. He was staring at her. She realized her skirts had ridden high up on her legs during the race from town. She returned the no-necked man's stare with as much defiance as she could muster and made no move to pull her skirt down.

"My, my," the man said with a lecherous wink, "this young filly's got one hell of a set of legs on her. Not bad nowhere else, either."

"Mind your tongue, Jeb Dawson!" The Preacher's scratchy voice seemed to deepen in sudden and thunderous rage. "Put carnal thoughts from your mind or suffer the wrath of the Creator's chosen!"

The man called Jeb Dawson lifted a hand. "No need to get all excited, Preacher. I was just makin' a little observation." Jeb's dark brown eyes glittered with obvious lust as he stared at Victoria.

Preacher ignored Jeb's comment. He turned to the youngest member of the group, a smooth-shaven man in his early twenties, the one who led the pack horses. "Dade, you've got the best horse in this bunch. Turn the pack animals over to Jeb. Go back up the trail a half mile or so and make sure we're not followed. We'll let the horses blow here for a few minutes. Follow and rejoin us when you are sure there is no pursuit."

Dade nodded, reined his horse about, and urged the leggy roan into a trot. Victoria watched him go, wondering. He seemed out of place in a gang of brutal cutthroats led by a madman.

The thought jarred her back to her own predicament. She had no way of knowing if the man called Preacher meant to keep her alive, as he had promised in the bank, or if he planned to kill her as soon as they were sure no one was following them. Or, perhaps, throw her to this pack of animals. The latter thought brought no special dread or fear. *There's not a hell of a lot they can do to me,* she told herself, *that would be worse than what I've lived through already.* She decided the best thing to do at the moment was to keep quiet until she could come up with some plan to escape.

The man named Dirk turned from the injured robber to Preacher. "Jubal's hit pretty hard." The voice was calm, matter-of-fact, and there was no expression in the smoky eyes. "I don't think he'll make it without a doctor."

"We will seek no aid in this state of sinners," Preacher said. "If he lives until we reach Cimarron, we will take him to a physician. If not, it is the will of the Almighty. Mount up, men. We'll be moving out now. We should reach Stinking Springs before sundown."

Jeb Dawson finally tore his gaze from Victoria's legs and motioned toward the bank bags tied to the horn of Preacher's saddle. "How much you reckon we got there, Preacher?"

The tall man patted one of the sacks. "Enough. There will be time to count it later, Jeb." Preacher twisted in the saddle to face Victoria. He smiled, a brief flash of chipped and stained teeth through the beard, but madness still glittered in his eyes. "Fear not, child," he said. "You will not be mistreated or

injured. Unless, of course, we are followed. Then I would kill
you as I promised. My word is my bond."

Victoria nodded without speaking. The night was still ahead.
She wondered if Preacher could control Jeb Dawson once they
had made camp. Or if he would even try.

The young man named Dade caught up with them two hours
later. "No sign of a posse," he said. "Not a rider anywhere in
sight."

"Good, good," Preacher said. He glanced over his shoulder
at Victoria. "Do not fret, child. You will be safe until we cross
the border into Mexico. Then you will be set free."

Victoria again nodded silently. It was a long way from here
to Mexico. There would be a time when escape was possible.
The *had* to be. Until then, it was a matter of patience—and
survival.

The group rode in silence through most of the day, the
moans of the wounded man the only human counterpoint to
the snort of horses, the creak of saddle leather, and the sigh
of the wind over the treeless, almost flat landscape.

The sun was two hours above the western horizon before
Preacher finally spoke. "The Lord has brought us in safety to
our destination," he said. A bony finger pointed toward the
dark green smear of a grove of stunted trees in a shallow valley
a mile away. "A way station. As the Good Book says, every
valley shall be exploited, every hill made low, and the straight
shall be made crooked."

The Preacher's biblical quotations were as warped as his
brain, Victoria thought. She phrased the verse from Isaiah
properly in her mind: *"Every valley shall be exalted, and
every mountain and hill shall be made low: and the crooked
shall be made straight, and the rough places plain: And the
glory of the Lord shall be revealed, and all flesh shall see it
together—"* The silent recitation brought a nervous flutter of
dread to her stomach. *All flesh will see it together. And that
damned Jeb Dawson is staring at me again—*

Stinking Springs was aptly named, Victoria thought as she
sat beside a small fire, her legs drawn up, knees cradled in her
elbows. The so-called spring was little more than a boggy seep

surrounded by sucking black mud that reeked of dead things and was home to swarms of bugs. But in the center of the muck was water, and in this part of southwestern Kansas anything wet was welcome. She longed for the clear well water of her hometown, her nightly bath. There would be no bath, she knew, but there would be night. She glanced at the lowering sun. *It won't be long,* she though, *until I know what they have planned for me.*

Clell Bates knelt beside Jubal's bedroll and wiped his friend's face with a soiled cloth dampened in the filthy ooze at the side of the seep. Jubal's sun browned face was pale, drawn into a mask of pain, and he shivered from the chill of a raging fever. Victoria thought he would probably die soon, but she admitted she knew almost nothing about gunshot wounds. At any rate, she told herself, he had gotten no worse nor better than he deserved.

She became aware that someone was watching her; she could almost feel the pressure of staring eyes. She slowly turned her head and gazed into the leering face of Jeb Dawson twenty feet away. The shudder in her belly returned. In the past few hours she had come to realize Dawson intended to have her, sooner or later. The trick was to delay it as long as possible—

"Miss Tucker?"

She turned away from Dawson. The young outlaw called Dade stood beside her, a tin plate filled with beans and bacon in his hand. "I brought you this. You should eat."

Victoria realized she was hungry—famished, in fact, despite all that had happened that day. She took the plate with a smile of thanks. Dade started to turn away.

"Mr. Dade? Would you mind sitting with me for a moment?"

The young man glanced about, as if confused and unsure how to react to the invitation, then squatted beside her. "Just call me Dade," he said. "My folks gave me two last names— Dade Fowler."

"You don't seem like the others," Victoria said, her tone soft and earnest. "It's as if you don't belong here at all." She lifted a forkful of beans and raised an eyebrow at the young outlaw.

"I—I guess maybe I don't, Miss Tucker," he said. His tone was wistful. "I joined up with Preacher and his band a few days back. I'm thinking now that it might have been a mistake." A frown creased his brow. He was, Victoria decided, a rather handsome young man, maybe even a decent and gentle sort, beneath the trail grime. "I killed a man up in Nebraska. I didn't want to, but it happened."

Victoria paused between bites. "Was it self-defense?"

"If it had been anyone else, yes," Dade said. "But the man happened to be the circuit judge's nephew."

"I see. And now you're in with a band of ruthless men led by an insane character who thinks he was put on the earth to do violence and murder in the name of the Lord."

Dade shook his head ruefully. "I can sure pick them, can't I?" He sighed. "Anyway, I've got to get to Mexico. I thought there was supposed to be safety in numbers. I was wrong. I'll be leaving them when I think I can do so without getting shot to pieces." He lowered his voice to a near whisper. "Watch out for Preacher, Miss Tucker. He's in his religious mood right now. But his mood can change at any minute. When it does, he turns into the meanest son of a—the meanest man I've ever seen. It's like there are two people inside him." Dade dropped his gaze. "Miss Tucker, I'm sorry you got pulled into this. Are you all right? Is there anything I can do?"

Victoria swallowed the last bite of bacon. "As a matter of fact, there is something," she said. "Riding astride in a dress is—well, it's rather uncomfortable, not to mention somewhat immodest. Would you happen to have some spare clothing I could borrow?"

The young man leapt to his feet. "Yes, Miss Tucker. I'll fetch it for you right now. It may not fit just right, but it should work."

"Thank you, Dade. And please—call me Victoria."

Dade's smile was genuine. "I'd be honored, Victoria. I'll be back in just a minute."

Victoria watched the young man hurry toward his packs. *That's one man I can bring over to my side,* she thought. *If he'll follow the carrot, I can use him, play him against the others, if I have to.* She felt no remorse about playing up to

Dade. In a battle for survival, anything was fair.

As promised, Dade returned a moment later, a shirt and pair of pants in his hands. "I'm afraid they're a little trail worn, Miss—Victoria."

Victoria smiled as she took the clothing. "Thank you, Dade. I'm sure they will be just fine. I'm in your debt." She glanced about. "If I only had some place to change in privacy." *And maybe a chance to run in the process,* she thought. She dismissed the idea as quickly as it formed. In the middle of this open prairie there was no place to hide, nowhere to run.

"I'll see what I can do," the young cowboy said.

A few minutes later, Preacher strode up to the young woman. "I will accompany you to a place where you may change clothing, child. You will be safe with me." He held up a hand. His fingernails were ragged and chipped. "These hands have no carnal urges, child. They have not touched female flesh since the Lord came to me." He pointed toward a cluster of low, scraggly bushes at the edge of camp.

Victoria made her way into the small thicket, found a spot where she would be screened from the rest of the camp, and reached for the top button of her dress. She glanced at Preacher, hoping he would turn his back.

He didn't.

The tall man stood and watched without comment as Victoria stripped the dress away and quickly donned the borrowed shirt and trousers. The pants were too large in the waist, but a bit snug in the hips. The pale blue cotton shirt strained to cover her breasts. Victoria noted with dismay that the thin material did not conceal the dark circles of her nipples; the one thing she did not want was to further excite the men—especially Jeb Dawson.

"Child," Preacher said as she tugged the high-topped, buttoned shoes onto her feet, "have you ever given yourself to a man?"

She glanced at the tall man, a sudden surge of fear pushing against her throat. "No, sir. I have never done that." *The answer is the truth,* Victoria thought. *I've never willingly shared my bed.*

Preacher nodded. A faint smile creased the stubbled face.

"I thought not, child. It's true, then, my vision. You *are* the virgin of Babylon! Child, you have my word that no man in this camp will molest you. If one should try, cry out, and the vengeance of the Almighty shall fall upon his head."

Victoria breathed a silent sigh of relief. At least for now she would be safe—unless Preacher changed as Dade had warned he might, or until one of his own men shot him. In the meantime, she decided, it was enough.

3

It seemed to Slocum that the whole population of Scott's Ford had turned out for the double funeral in the windswept cemetery on the northwest side of town. The man Slocum had killed in the bank shoot-out would be buried later in the pauper's corner of the county cemetery. Slocum didn't expect a big turnout for that one.

The services for Katie and the bank teller named Curry had been mercifully brief. Will Tucker's wife had openly and without shame shed tears for both, and tried her best to comfort Curry's widow, his daughter, and the children. Tucker himself had stood with no outward expression as the first shovel of dirt fell on Curry's grave.

Now the crowd began to filter from the graveyard back to their own lives. Slocum stood for a moment over Katie's grave, hat in hand. *It was my fault, Katie. If I hadn't been in town, if you hadn't been with me yesterday morning, if I had been quicker, if I could have pushed you out of the way—God, girl, I'm sorry. Try to forgive me if you can hear me.*

For an instant Slocum thought he heard Katie's husky laugh. Then he realized it was only the wind in the tall prairie grass. He turned away, pulled his hat down against the freshening breeze, and strode back toward town.

Those men would die, Slocum vowed anew. They would die hard, and they would know why. The ache of loss and hurt and the weight of his own guilt began to fade under a fresh wave of cold, hard rage as Slocum strode into the lobby of the Exchange Hotel. He had barely enough money to pay the board bill for himself and his horses, and no prospect of more to come. But he would find a way. He could live off the land if he had to. He had done it before.

"Mr. Slocum?"

Slocum turned at the call. Will Tucker stood by a chair in the lobby. The banker's wife sat in the chair, her back straight, her eyes red-rimmed but dry, head held high despite the emotional strain of the funerals and the unknown fate of her daughter. *This lady has class,* Slocum thought; *I just wonder if her husband has as much.* He touched fingers to his hat brim in greeting to the woman.

"Mr. Slocum, my wife and I would like to discuss something with you—a business proposal of sorts."

"Before we begin, Mr. Slocum," the banker's wife said, "please permit me to express my condolences on your loss. Katie was a sweet person, always happy and full of life. We will miss her greatly."

Slocum nodded. "Thank you, Mrs. Tucker."

"Mr. Slocum," Tucker said, "we have had some responses from those telegrams you sent out." He handed a sheaf of papers to Slocum. Slocum thumbed through the messages. The bandits fit the descriptions of the outlaws known as the Whiteside gang.

Slocum tucked the folded messages in his pocket. "The tall man, the leader of the gang, is Eldon Whiteside, also known as Preacher," Slocum said. "He doesn't have all the aces in his deck. Crazy as a loon." He frowned. "I've heard of the Whiteside bunch. Word is they hit a mine payroll and killed three men outside of Deadwood a few weeks back, then robbed a bank in Nebraska a spell after that. Tough men, most of them on somebody's wanted list."

"Any indication as to the identities of the others?" Mrs. Tucker asked.

Slocum tapped a finger against the messages in his pocket. "The man I killed—the one with the shotgun—was Lloyd Kinnebrew, an escapee from the federal penitentiary in

Leavenworth. He was supposed to hang for murder this week. A new member of the clan, apparently. There are supposed to be from six to ten of them. No one seems to know for sure. Nobody I wired could put a last name to the one-eyed man I put a couple of slugs into."

Tucker paused and ran a finger across his jaw. "Mr. Slocum, these men have my daughter. God only knows what those—those *animals*—will do to her."

"Will," Mrs. Tucker interrupted, "you're talking around the issue. Mr. Slocum, we would like to employ you to rescue Victoria."

"Mrs. Tucker, I've never been a gun for hire—"

"I'm aware of that, sir," she interrupted. "I sent out some inquiries of my own. I am also aware that you have a considerable reputation as a gunman, and that you are a man with the talent and courage to track down a ruthless gang like those outlaws."

Slocum took a long, hard look at the woman's face. Her gold-flecked brown eyes held a calm but determined expression, the line of her jaw set and firm. *A strong woman,* Slocum thought. *A woman who knows what she wants and gets straight to the point. I like her.*

"Mrs. Tucker, I was about to say that my gun is not for hire, but as far as I know, only ten rules have ever been carved in stone." He heard the tight anger in his tone. "I may have broken most of those Ten Commandments during my life, but I never break a promise. I made a promise to Katie."

"Mr. Slocum, I don't doubt for a moment you will fulfill that promise. Lord knows, you deserve your vengeance. But our concern is getting our daughter back alive and unharmed. Will you consider helping us?"

Slocum pondered the proposal for a moment, then nodded. "I will. As long as I'm free to work in my own way."

"Good, Slocum," the banker said with a sigh of relief. "Name your price. I'll pay it to get my little girl back. And, of course, any of the bank's money you can recover."

Slocum glared at the banker until Tucker dropped his gaze. "The bank's money, Mr. Tucker, is not a hell of a lot of concern to me. Those men are—that and getting your daughter out alive."

"Gentlemen, please," Mrs. Tucker said firmly, "this is no time to quibble." She turned the full force of her gaze on Slocum. The impact was considerable. "Mr. Slocum, I would appreciate an honest answer. In your opinion, what are your chances of bringing Victoria home alive?"

Slocum ran a thumb along his jaw in thought for several heartbeats. Then he sighed. "To be brutally honest, Mrs. Tucker, the chances are slim. If those men know they're being followed, they'll kill her on the spot. And from what I've heard of that bunch, they may kill her anyway when they feel safe." He waved a hand toward the window. "It's a big country out there. It could take days, maybe weeks. And that might be too long for Victoria." Slocum paused for a breath. "Mrs. Tucker, I hate to bring this up, but it's something we have to face. If and when I bring Victoria home, she may not be the same girl she was."

Mrs. Tucker listened without wincing. "I'm aware of that, Mr. Slocum. We will deal with that situation when it arises. On the matter of funds, we will advance any amount you request— within reason, of course—for expenses. Upon my daughter's safe return, we will pay you five hundred dollars, plus your own three hundred that was taken."

Slocum nodded his acceptance. "I'll need a hundred to begin with, and the authority to wire for more, if need be. I may have to buy some information along the way, and that's something that doesn't always come cheap."

"Agreed." Tucker stepped to Slocum and thrust out a hand. "And, while my daughter's safe return is the primary objective, if you are able to recover any of the money taken from the bank, we will pay you a bonus of ten percent of the amount returned. Is that satisfactory?"

"It is." Slocum accepted the banker's handshake. "I can get the supplies I need today and be on their trail by sunup tomorrow."

"How many men do you need? There are a few in town I could recommend."

"I work alone, Mr. Tucker." Slocum released Tucker's hand and turned to the banker's wife.

"Mrs. Tucker, I need to know as much as you can tell me about Victoria—her personality, habits, anything that could be of value when—if I'm able to reach her."

Slocum listened intently as Mrs. Tucker described Victoria. She had been a bubbly, outgoing child, with a quick mind, intelligent beyond her years, but otherwise a normal, healthy young girl.

"Then, something seemed to happen," Mrs. Tucker said. "I have no idea what. But shortly after her first—after she became a woman—she changed. She stopped smiling and laughing. It was as if she had retreated into some world of her own."

Slocum glanced at Will Tucker. The banker suddenly seemed uncomfortable. He shifted his feet and was unwilling to meet Slocum's gaze. "It was a sudden change, then?" Slocum asked.

"Very sudden. Victoria—matured, I suppose, is the proper word—rather early, Mr. Slocum. She was not yet thirteen when she became a woman." While her husband seemed embarrassed or bothered with the conversation, Mrs. Tucker appeared merely confused. "She had always been a loving child, quick with a hug or a kiss. And then, in the course of just a few weeks, she became withdrawn, cool and distant. She seemed to cringe from a touch, which wasn't like her at all. Sometimes in the morning it appeared she hadn't slept at all. Her eyes would be red as though she had been crying, but she would never tell me what was wrong."

Slocum nodded, mulling over the information. Whatever had happened must have been sudden and painful, he thought. People changed; it was the nature of the beast. But they didn't change almost overnight.

"If you two will excuse me," Tucker said, "I'll go get Mr. Slocum his money. When you're finished here, Mr. Slocum, I'll be at the bank." He donned his hat, nodded to Slocum, and strode from the hotel.

The banker's wife watched him go, then turned back to Slocum. "Please try to understand, Mr. Slocum," she said, "it's not that my husband is obsessed by money. In fact, he would pay his last dime to have our daughter back. She's our only child, and he loves her so." She sighed. "On the other hand, we've worked so hard to build our bank business and the reputation of the institution. Most of the people from three counties around keep their funds in our bank. Those people won't lose a dime; we will see to that. The robbers got away with a considerable sum, but not all the money that was on deposit. Will keeps most of the hard currency in a small safe beneath the floorboards under his desk. The big one is something of a decoy. What we did lose, however, will hurt. Not only our personal finances, but our reputation." The expression in her eyes hardened. "Those men also must pay for the death of poor Mr. Curry. He was a good man. He had been with us for ten years, and he was like one of the family."

"I understand, Mrs. Tucker." He inclined his head, as near to a bow of respect as Slocum ever showed. "I'd better get busy. There's a lot to be done before sunup." He started to turn away, then paused. "Mrs. Tucker, did Victoria have any young male friends?"

The woman's brow furrowed. "Only one. A young man who arrived here only a short time ago from back East. A polite young man named Link. He has the strangest eyes, sort of an amber color. Most unusual."

Slocum frowned. "I believe we've met," he said. "There were no others? Your daughter is a beautiful young woman, Mrs. Tucker. I'd think every young man in town would be courting her."

Mrs. Tucker shook her head, obviously puzzled. "I thought so, too, but Victoria would have nothing to do with them. Link was the only one she showed even the slightest interest in, and they did nothing but sit in the parlor and talk and occasionally share a pot of chocolate. They never left the house together, even to go riding." She blinked against the pain of the memory. "Riding was Victoria's only indulgence, Mr. Slocum. She's quite a good horsewoman."

"Thank you, Mrs. Tucker," Slocum said. He turned to walk away.

"Mr. Slocum?"

Slocum glanced over his shoulder. "Yes?"

"Bring my daughter back."

"I'll do my best, Mrs. Tucker."

Slocum stepped into the street and strode toward the bank. He fought back the impulse to go straight to the stable, saddle up, and take to the trail. Patience had never been one of his long suits, except when he was on the final stalk. And he was a long way from that at the moment.

Slocum sat on the edge of his bed in the Exchange Hotel and tried to ignore the scent Katie had left behind. It was a faint but distinct smell, a hint of lilac water and woman and sweaty, spent sex. The scent lay like an indictment on Slocum's tongue.

On the bedside table one of Slocum's Colts lay stripped for cleaning. The second handgun, already cleaned, oiled, and fully loaded, lay within arm's reach on the rumpled sheets. His rifle, a Winchester model 76, rested in the saddle boot beside packs now filled with supplies for the long trail ahead. The rifle, like his handguns, was .44-40 caliber. There were more powerful long guns on the market, but this one had its advantages to Slocum. One was that the same ammunition fit both his rifle and his pistols. Another was that Slocum knew the weapon shot where it pointed. That was the only thing that really mattered when the last card in the poker game hit the table.

Buying supplies for the hunt had eaten half the hundred-dollar expense advance Will Tucker had provided, but Slocum was satisfied that he had all he would need. Now all he had to do was care for his weapons and try to get some sleep before saddling up at dawn.

Slocum doubted he would sleep much. There were too many fresh memories in that bed—

He swept the loaded Colt from the bed as a knock sounded on the door. He eared back the hammer, trained the muzzle on the middle of the doorway, and called, "Come in."

The young man with amber eyes pushed the door open, his hands held palm out, well away from the new Colt at his belt. The strange eyes held a gleam of desperation and pain. "Mr. Slocum, you've got to take me with you," the youth said.

Slocum stared at the youth named Link for a long moment, then lowered the muzzle of his Colt. "What the hell are you talking about, son?"

"You're going after those men. Mr. Tucker told me."

"Dammit," Slocum growled, "I told Tucker, and now I'll tell you. I work alone." He nodded toward the door. "Get out of here. Go back and play gunfighter with those fool friends of yours in the saloon. You're sure as hell not going with me."

Link's face flushed in shame. "Look, Mr. Slocum, I'm sorry about that business the other night. I—I was drunk. I didn't know what I was doing—"

"That was pretty damned obvious," Slocum interrupted with a snort of disgust.

"They—those two egged me on. They kept telling me how fast I was. I realize now I was a fool." The note of apology faded; a tone of urgency edged back in the young man's voice. "Please, Mr. Slocum. You've *got* to take me along."

"No." Slocum put the Colt back at his side and reached for a lightly oiled cloth. He began to wipe the sear assembly of the dismantled pistol.

"I have money. I'll pay you."

Slocum glared at Link. He made no attempt to disguise the disgust in his stare. "What part of the word *no* do you have trouble understanding?"

Link's face flushed again, but this time it seemed to be a rush of anger, Slocum noted. "Mr. Slocum, those men have Victoria."

"That's not exactly news."

"Dammit, Slocum!" The youth's voice had a sharp edge to it now. "Have you ever loved anybody—anybody at all—in your life?"

Slocum sighed, put down the pieces of the Colt, and looked again into Link's amber eyes. He saw the pleading there, and the flicker of fear. "What's that got to do with anything?"

"I love that girl, Mr. Slocum. I've been going crazy, thinking about—about what they might do to her. Christ, they might even kill her." The youth dropped his gaze again. "Mr. Slocum, I couldn't live with that. If something happened to Victoria, and I didn't even try to help her—" His voice trailed away.

"Link," Slocum said, "if it's any comfort, I know how you feel. But look at it from my side. Those are dangerous men. They kill people, sometimes just for the pure hell of it. They'll kill Victoria for certain if they think they're being followed. Now, it's going to be hard enough for one man to track them down and get Victoria back. If anybody can do that, I can." He paused for a moment to emphasize his next words. "I can't do it with a greenhorn along. Son, I don't know much about you, except that you seem to be in a hurry to get dead. That's your problem. But I'm not letting you take me, and Victoria, with you. I can't watch out for those hard cases and keep your nose wiped at the same time. Is that clear enough?"

Link stood for a moment in silence. "All right, Mr. Slocum, I'll freely admit my shortcomings. I'm young, and as you say, I'm green—new to the West and its ways. But I'll learn."

"No."

Link sighed. "All right, Mr. Slocum. If you won't take me along, I'll follow you. Every time you look over your shoulder, I'll be there. And I'll stay there until Victoria is safe."

Link turned toward the door. Slocum's jaw muscles bunched in anger. The kid was just enough of a damn fool to try to follow—and get everybody killed in the process. "Link," he called.

The youth turned back toward Slocum, hope flaring in the amber eyes. "Yes?"

"Like I said, the last thing I need is a greenhorn tagging along. But if you're bound and determined to get yourself killed, you might as well do it right. Can you keep your mouth shut when I say so, do what I tell you when I tell you to do it, and keep out of my way the rest of the time?"

Link nodded. "I can do that. I won't be a problem, Mr. Slocum."

"I doubt that, son. But if I'm going to be saddled with you, at least it will be where I can keep an eye on you instead of trying to watch ahead and behind at once." Slocum sighed in resignation. *The skunk's in the henhouse now,* he grumbled to himself, *and I've got to sweep up the feathers.* He glared at Link. "Tracking men takes money. I have only enough supplies for myself."

"I'll get my own, Mr. Slocum. As I said, I have money. Now I'll ask your help for the first time. What supplies will I need?"

Slocum quickly ran down the list, from a pack horse that could double as an extra mount to grub and ammunition. "Do you have a rifle?" he concluded.

Link nodded.

"Make sure you have plenty of cartridges. At least fifty for the rifle, a hundred for the handgun. I hope to high heaven you can use a long gun better than you handle a revolver." Slocum made no effort to keep the sarcasm from his tone.

"I can, sir," the young man said confidently. "You may think I'm a complete idiot with firearms after that stupid display of mine in the saloon, but I assure you, I can handle a rifle. I've been around them most of my life."

Slocum snorted in disbelief. "That couldn't have been very long," he said. "How old are you, by the way?"

"Seventeen, Mr. Slocum. Eighteen in a few weeks."

"I see. All right, Link. You better get a move on. Get your supplies bought and be ready to hit the trail at first light. I'll be at the stable at sunup. Be ready, or you stay behind."

Link nodded. "I'll be ready." He turned toward the door.

"Link? I'll likely need something to put on your headstone before this is over. What's your full name?"

The youth's face reddened again. "You'll laugh."

Slocum reached out and put his hand on the Colt revolver at his side. "On Slocum's Bible here, I'll swear. I won't laugh."

"My full name, sir, is Ulysses Grant Abraham Lincoln."

Slocum stared at him for a moment. "Damn, son," he finally said, "if I'd known that before, I'd have been tempted to go ahead and kill you back in that saloon."

Link's face turned beet-red in anger. "You said you wouldn't laugh at me, Slocum."

"I'm not laughing." Slocum stared straight into the youth's amber eyes. "I fought on the other side." He shrugged. "What the hell. The war's over. Just do me a favor."

"What might that be?"

"Stay alive. It would take me a week to carve all that on a gravestone. For now," Slocum said, "Link will do just fine for a name."

"And you, Slocum? What would go on your headstone?"

"Slocum. That's all." A wry grin touched his lips. "But after this, you might add the words, 'He was a little stupid.' Go on, Link, and get your stuff together. I'll see you at sunup."

Slocum waited until the door closed behind Ulysses Grant Abraham Lincoln, then shook his head. "And what part of the word *no*," he asked himself aloud, "don't you understand yourself, Slocum?"

"Good God, Link!" Slocum stared at the young man's tack in astonishment. "What the hell is that?"

The pale first light of early dawn set a glow against more silver than Slocum had seen since his last big poker game in Denver. The black leather of Link's saddle sparkled with dozens of silver conchos; broad corner swatches of engraved German silver adorned the rounded flanks of the saddle skirt; and what appeared to be a solid silver plate ran from bit bar to browband on a flashy headstall, dyed black to match the saddle.

"Why, my saddle and bridle, of course," Link said, confused. "What did you think it is?"

Slocum snorted in genuine disgust. "A damn lighthouse, that's what. When the sun hits that silver, a man could see you coming for twenty miles. Get rid of it."

Link looked at the rig as if seeing it for the first time. "Oh. I see what you mean. What should I do?"

Slocum waved toward a small tack room in the stable. "Hostler's got a plain rig in there. Double-cinch stock saddle without any fancy stuff on it. Take it and leave yours in its place."

Slocum shook his head as he watched the young man hurry to strip the silver-studded saddle from the leggy black gelding and carry the rig toward the stable. Slocum saddled his own mount, then adjusted the packs on the stocky bay. The bay tried to take a nip from Slocum's shoulder. He cuffed the horse on the neck with an open hand. The game was over for one more day.

Satisfied with his own preparations, Slocum looked Link's mount over and decided the kid might be green as grass, but it was obvious he knew horses. The black was trim, well muscled, and gentle but alert, with an intelligent look in its eyes. The horse appeared to have plenty of speed and staying power.

The animal Link had chosen as a pack horse wasn't as flashy as the black, but he would do. The star-faced brown was big, about sixteen hands, broad-chested and deep of girth, and heavily muscled. Probably not much for speed, Slocum thought, but hell for stout, and a man never knew when a powerful horse might come in handy.

Link emerged from the stable, tossed the scarred and trail-worn stock saddle into place, and cinched up. The stock of a rifle protruded from the concho-studded black scabbard slung beneath the right stirrup. Slocum followed as Link stepped around the horse, produced a pocketknife, pried the conchos from the saddle boot, and tossed them aside. Then he raised an eyebrow at Slocum. "That better?"

"A lot. Remember how much better every time you don't get shot." He nodded toward the rifle stock. "What kind of long gun are you packing?"

"Forty-five-ninety Winchester."

Slocum's lips pursed in a silent whistle. "That's a lot of rifle. Can you use it?"

"It shoots where it's pointed. Kicks like a Missouri mule, but it'll stop anything smaller than a Union Pacific locomotive," Link said. "I can use it."

Slocum glanced at the eastern horizon. The sun was half a handspan into the sky. "All right, son. Mount up. We've got a long way to go today."

Slocum led the way as the two men rode out, horses moving at a steady, ground-eating trot. A mile outside of Scott's Ford, Slocum reined his sorrel from the road.

"Why turn off here?" Link asked.

"Because they did."

"How do you know that?"

Slocum waved a hand toward the grass beneath them. "Five horses moving fast leave a wide trail, Link. Look around. See how the grass is bent, watch for hoofprints in the bare spots." Slocum leaned in the saddle to study the mark of a hoof in a break in the grass. "They were still running their mounts here.

When the toe of a hoof digs in deep like this, you know the horse was moving fast."

Link nodded silently. "Hope you don't mind my asking, Mr. Slocum. This tracking business is new to me."

"Keep your eyes and ears open, Link," Slocum said, "and before this is over, you'll be able to track a cottontail rabbit over solid rock."

The two rode in silence for another mile, then Link abruptly checked his mount. He leaned down, studied the leaves of a stand of tall bunch grass, then glanced at Slocum. "There's blood on some of the leaves."

"Probably from the man I shot," Slocum said. "You're learning."

"Where do you think they're headed?"

"Mexico, most likely," Slocum said.

"How do you figure that?"

"It's where I would go if I was on the run." Slocum's gaze swept the almost flat landscape ahead. He saw no human sign.

More than two hours passed before Link broke the silence. "Slocum, when will we catch up with them?"

"That's the scorpion in our pants," Slocum said, his brow furrowed. "If we catch up too quick—and they see us after them—they'll kill the girl. So we'll move up slow and easy, take whatever hand we're dealt, and play the cards as best we can."

"What will happen to Victoria in the meantime?" Slocum could hear the anguish in the young man's voice.

"I don't know, Link. Try not to think about it. That's the only way to stay sane in a game like this."

4

Victoria woke with a start from her fitful sleep, momentarily disoriented; instead of the canopy of her own bed above, a blanket of stars covered the Kansas sky.

Reality crashed back into her mind, pushed aside the grainy feeling in her tired eyes. She fought back the quick surge of panic, and the fleeting hope that she might find a chance to escape. Beside a small fire a few feet away, the man called Jeb Dawson squatted, coffee cup in hand, and stared at her.

Victoria lay on the blankets beside the man called Preacher. It had been his idea, not hers. "Come lie beside me, child," he had said, "and you will be safe from these other men. As one of the Lord's chosen, I no longer have need for the flesh of woman."

Once during the night Victoria had awakened as Preacher, tossing in his sleep, had let a hand fall across her breast. She had steeled herself for the worst as the coarse fingers closed around and squeezed her breast; then the Preacher seemed to jerk awake and he snatched his hand from her body as if he had touched a hot rock. *What he said was true,* Victoria thought. *He feels nothing but revulsion toward me as a woman.* The idea was not especially reassuring. It might keep her from being assaulted for the time being, but it was another sign of the insanity of the man beside her. She wondered for a moment what could have caused the crazy man to feel that way, then dismissed the puzzle from her mind. At the moment it was enough; for now she was beyond the reach of the stocky man by the fire.

The buzz of night insects, the cry of a hunting owl, and the snores of sleeping men hummed through the night air, punctuated by the moans and labored breathing of the wounded man. The air was heavy with the foul odor of Stinking Springs. Victoria sighed, reached for sleep, and found it beyond her grasp. She turned onto her side, her back to Preacher. At least, she reminded herself, she could rest, even if she could not sleep—

The sound of boots crunching on sand brought her head around.

Jeb Dawson stood above her, his breathing heavy. In the darkness she could not make out the expression on his face, but could imagine the glitter of lust in the dark brown eyes. Jeb squatted on his heels at her side and probed thick, coarse fingers beneath the blanket. His left hand settled on her stomach. His fingers slipped beneath the waistband of her borrowed pants. "Just one feel won't hurt nobody, sis," Jeb said. "I want to know what kinda bush you got down there."

A sudden flare of anger and disgust swept aside the fear that knotted Victoria's belly. "Take your hands off me, you dirty son of a bitch, or I'll tear your balls off." Her tone was icy despite the softness of her voice.

She thought she could see a gleam in Jeb's eyes in the darkness broken only by thin starlight. She heard his soft chuckle. "Damn if you ain't got spirit, sis," he said. "I like that in a filly. Makes 'em buck harder before they get broke to saddle." The stubby fingers moved downward.

Victoria doubled the fist at her side and slammed her knuckles into the man's crotch. She couldn't generate much leverage, but it was enough; Jeb cried out at the unexpected, intense pain—and then starlight flashed off metal, something heavy cracked into the side of Jeb's head, and he dropped onto the sand beside her. Victoria started at the sudden movement, then realized Preacher was sitting up, a long-barreled pistol in his hand.

Preacher reached across Victoria and whipped the pistol across the downed man's head again. The crack of steel on skull brought the camp awake within seconds.

Preacher tossed aside the blankets, cursing fluently, and stepped over Victoria's body to the unconscious Jeb. He thumbed the big pistol to full cock and aimed the muzzle at the back of Jeb's head.

"Preacher, no!" The yell from Clell Bates seemed to check Preacher's rage. "Don't! We need him!" The gun muzzle wavered, then dropped, only to whip back again and slash into the side of Jeb's head.

"You dare touch the virgin of Babylon, you unholy bastard?" Preacher's voice thundered in rage. "You were warned!" The pistol cracked against Jeb's head again. Then a hand reached out, grasped Preacher's bony wrist, and held firm.

"That's enough," Clell Bates said. "No need to pistol-whip Jeb to death. I reckon he's learned his lesson. Remember, he's the one best knows the trail to Helltown. We need him, Preacher. We need him alive."

The killing rage seemed to drain from the tall man. He holstered the pistol and stood for a moment, staring down at the crumpled outlaw. Other members of the band gathered around, glancing warily at each other, then at Preacher, then at the man on the ground. In the faint starlight Victoria could see the black smear of blood on Jeb's head and shoulders.

"No man here shall lay a hand on this child," Preacher all but shouted. "I will tolerate no whoring in the camp of the Lord!" Preacher's shoulders lifted and fell as the last of his rage faded. "Clell, tend to this sinner. Perhaps when he regains his senses he will see the error of his ways."

Preacher watched as Clell Bates and the lean man with Indian features dragged Jeb toward the fire. Then Preacher turned to Victoria.

"Are you all right, child? Did he harm you?"

Victoria shook her head. "No, sir. You stopped him in time. For that, I thank you. I am in your debt."

Preacher placed a bony hand on Victoria's shoulder. "I am but following the Almighty's word, child. 'The man who keeps unsoiled the virgin of Babylon shall find his reward in heaven and his peace upon the face of the Earth,' as the Good Book says. You will not be harmed as long as you remain at my side." The thin man's voice tightened. "Unless we are followed and I am forced to take your life, I will observe that covenant." Preacher glanced toward the stars. "It's only a couple of hours until dawn. Since the camp is aroused, we might as well prepare for the day." He waved a hand at young Dade Fowler. Victoria noted for the first time that Dade's hand rested on the grips of his pistol. "Dade, fuel the fire and tend to the horses. We will breakfast, then ride at first light."

"Yes, sir." Dade turned toward the fire, then paused. "Preacher, we can rearrange the packs and free up one of the horses for Miss Tucker to ride," he said. "That would make it a lot easier on your horse."

Preacher stared for a moment at Victoria. "Child, do I have your word you will not try to flee?"

Victoria nodded.

"Very well. Dade, pick the slowest of the mounts for her. If she should then be tempted, it would be an easy matter to run her down."

Victoria flashed a quick smile of thanks to Dade, but she wasn't sure he saw the gesture in the darkness. At least now she would be more comfortable. It would be easier riding alone; she could maintain some control over her mount and her own balance—and after a full day of riding double behind the unwashed tall man in the battered top hat, the simple scent of horse and dust would be a relief.

The sun was past its midpoint before Preacher signaled the noon halt for the day in a waterless swale amid the rolling, sandy grassland. Victoria sensed that they were somewhere deep in southwest Kansas, but she didn't know the country and couldn't be sure. She had overheard someone mention reaching the Cimarron Strip before nightfall.

She slid from the back of the borrowed pack horse and stood for a moment on legs left weak by the long ride. She might be uncomfortable, she thought, but she was in a lot better shape than the wounded man, Jubal. Clell had been riding alongside Jubal, holding him in the saddle. Jubal begged almost constantly for water when he wasn't slumped half-conscious over the saddle horn, moaning in constant agony. She watched as Clell eased the wounded man from the saddle and helped him sit.

Preacher knelt beside Jubal, examined the wounds again, and shook his head.

The scrape of a boot behind her brought Victoria around with a start.

Jeb Dawson, the cuts on his face still seeping blood, one eye swollen shut, and puffy bruises showing blue-black against his swarthy skin, stood glaring at her.

"I'll get you for this, you little bitch," Dawson muttered through swollen and split lips. "I'll take you, and when I'm through with you, I'll ram the barrel of my pistol up your pussy and pull the trigger."

Victoria suppressed a shudder and glared back at the swarthy outlaw, trying not to let her fear of the man show. She could tell by the tone of his voice that Dawson was totally serious about the threat.

"You can't hide behind Preacher forever, sis," Dawson half whispered. "He'll change or get killed, and then you're mine."

Victoria stood in silence as the pistol-whipped outlaw stomped away. *I've got to get away from here,* she thought in a flush of panic, *or find a weapon of some sort.* She glanced toward the crown of the swale they had just crossed. There had been no sign of life on their back trail, but Victoria knew someone would be following. Her father wasn't going to just let her go, even if he got her killed in the process. *Dear old Dad,* she told herself bitterly, *is not going to let anyone make off with his little girl; he's got other plans for her. I just hope that whoever might be out there is good at what he does.*

Slocum knelt at the edge of the boggy seep and studied the signs, then glanced up at Link.

"God," Link said, "this place smells to high heaven."

"That's why they call it Stinking Springs, Link," Slocum said. "They were here. Camped overnight."

Link swung down from his black, studied the campsite, then knelt to trace a finger around one small footprint. "Victoria's tracks," he said, his voice low. "She's wearing those high-button shoes. I wonder what happened here—" His voice trailed away.

Slocum stood. "Don't fret over it, Link. At least she's still alive. Or was at this camp." He squinted toward the sun. It was a double handspan over the western horizon. "We'll stay here for the night."

"Why, for Christ's sake?" Link's tone was one of disbelief. "There's still better than two hours of daylight left. We could track them another five or six miles."

Slocum shrugged. "Our horses need water. This is it for the next day and a half, until we hit the Cimarron. The first thing you've got to learn, Link, is to take care of your horse. It's a hell of a long walk from here to anywhere. The next thing you learn is patience. Have you ever done any hunting?"

"Quite a lot, back in Pennsylvania and Ohio. Deer and squirrel, mostly. My father took me moose hunting a few times in upstate Maine."

Slocum pulled a cigarillo from his pocket, fired it with a lucifer, and raised an eyebrow at Link. "What we're doing is sort of the same, except deer and squirrels don't shoot back. We take it slow on the trail, even slower on the stalk, and then make the first shot count. Which reminds me that if I'm going to make a pistolero out of you, we best get started as soon as we tend the horses."

Slocum unsaddled his mount and stripped the packs off the bay, rubbed the geldings down with a pad of burlap and led them through the muck of the seep to drink from the fresher water. He kept a close eye on Link in the process, and was reasonably well satisfied at what he saw. The youngster watched and duplicated Slocum's motions with only a few minor mistakes and one solid blunder.

"Never hobbled a horse before, Link?" Slocum didn't try to hide the amusement in his voice. Link's pack horse stood with the hobbles strapped above the knees. Slocum could swear he could see a confused expression in the brown's eyes.

"No. Did I do something wrong?"

"Your horse seems to think so. He's not used to wearing a corset."

Link looked as confused as the horse. "Hobbles go above the fetlocks, son. Not above the knees. A horse can't move at all with his knees tied together."

"Oh. Sorry."

"Apologize to the horse, not me."

Link unbuckled the hobbles from above the brown's knees and refastened them in the proper place. The horse looked relieved, Slocum thought.

The sun was still well above the horizon when the horses were tended, fed, and left to graze in the rich grass near the seep.

Slocum prowled through the outlaws' campsite and came up with several empty cans. The finds disgusted Slocum. He had always believed a man should leave a camp in at least as good a condition as he found it. He motioned to Link. The greenhorn followed as Slocum strode around the seep to the far side, where the gentle rise of a low hill provided a backdrop.

Slocum placed two cans upright on the ground, tossed the others aside for the moment, and walked back ten paces. He nodded to Link. "Let's see what you can do with that handgun now, son," he said.

"Won't the outlaws hear the gunshots?"

"They're so far ahead of us they wouldn't hear Gabriel's trumpet," Slocum said. He nodded toward the Colt strapped low on Link's thigh. "Show me what you can do."

Link flexed his knees, fingers twitching above the butt of the new Colt, his amber eyes fixed on the target. He yanked at the Colt. The gun cleared leather, spun from Link's hand and fell with a thud on his right instep.

Slocum chuckled softly as Link yelped in surprise and pain. He hopped on one foot, trying to massage the sting from the bruise. His face turned a bright scarlet as embarrassment pushed aside the pain in his instep. He muttered a quiet curse and bent to retrieve the Colt.

"Guess I've got more to learn than I thought," Link said sheepishly as he glanced at Slocum.

"You might say that," Slocum said. He tried and failed to keep the grin from his face. "Wipe the dirt off the handgun and try again."

Link brushed away the sand, holstered the Colt, and went into his gunfighter stance, his eyes squinted at the target. He drew the pistol awkwardly, thrust the barrel toward the can, and swept the heel of his free hand across the hammer three times. One of the slugs kicked dirt six feet from the can. The other two missed the hillside completely.

"Jesus Christ, Link," Slocum said, unable to decide whether to laugh or cry, "where on God's green earth did you learn about gunfighting?"

Link's face colored anew. "I read a lot of books back East. Books about gunfighters."

"Penny dreadfuls and dime novels, you mean?"

"I've heard them called that."

"Forget everything you've read," Slocum said, "and especially that nonsense about fanning the hammer. I met a man once who fanned a handgun."

"Was he fast?"

"He got off four rounds to my two. One of his slugs hit the floor, one hit the ceiling, one went out the door and killed a horse at the hitch rail outside. The last one hit an innocent bystander in the arm. The bystander was a good forty feet off to the side of the shooter."

"What happened to him? The shooter, I mean. You said you fired twice."

Slocum shrugged. "Once probably would have been enough. The county paid for his funeral." Slocum nodded toward the untouched cans. "That hill over there could have killed you twice. If you want to ride with me, you'll learn to use that weapon the right way. I won't have a man at my side I can't depend on in a fight." Slocum sighed. "Reload and try it again. And this time, don't fan the hammer or I'll take that gun away from you before you kill a horse or something."

Link tried again. He fumbled for an instant with the hammer before he finally managed to yank off a shot. Dirt kicked from the slope five feet from the nearest can.

"Don't worry about speed, Link," Slocum said. "A lot of fast guns get dead. Speed doesn't mean squat it you can't put the slug where it'll do you some good and the other man considerable harm. Try it again, without the draw this time. Just aim and fire."

Link aimed and fired. The slug again landed well short of the mark.

"Don't yank the trigger, Link. Squeeze it."

Link nodded. The boy's jaw was set in determination. "Think smooth, Link. Let the gun flow, like an extension of your arm. Use the sights. Put the front blade in the center of the rear sight notch, right at the bottom of the target. That's called a six o'clock hold. When it feels right, squeeze the trigger."

Link's next shot came within a foot of the can. Slocum grunted in satisfaction. "That's better. Now, try two more. Remember, think smooth."

Link's .45 bellowed gray-white smoke. One slug kicked dirt near the side of the can, but the second ripped into the ground three feet over the top of the target.

Slocum sighed inwardly, but tried to keep his expression from showing his disapproval. "Let's take it from the basics this time, Link. Reload. We'll work from the draw."

Slocum stood behind and to the right of Link as the youngster reloaded and holstered the weapon. "First off," Slocum said, "let's get that Colt off your kneecap. You're carrying it way too low. Raise the gun belt up until the pistol grips are about the level of your hipbone."

Link didn't argue. He pulled the belt up around his hips and snugged it into place. "Now," Slocum said, "relax. If your muscles are tense, you have to unlock them before you can move your arm. Don't try to be fast on the draw, just smooth. Let your bottom three fingers wrap around the grips. Then, as the gun starts to clear leather, drop your index finger through the trigger guard and hook your thumb around the hammer. Pull the hammer back as the barrel starts up and let your thumb slide onto the backstrap. Give that a try without firing a shot."

Link's draw was still slow and awkward, Slocum noted, but it was a start. At least the kid had good reflexes. "Better, Link. Keep trying—and remember, think smooth. Don't rush it."

Fifteen minutes later, Link had the basics of the draw under control. He was still slow as February molasses, Slocum observed silently, but at least he wasn't likely to blow his own kneecap off. "Okay, now we'll try live fire. Draw and fire three rounds. Hold the grips firm but not hard. Don't fight the recoil; let it work for you. The grips of a single action Army are designed so that the recoil of the shot pushes the grips down in your hand and leaves your thumb in position to cock for another round. Ready?"

Link nodded.

"Go," Slocum said.

Link's first shot hit within inches of the can, his second kicked dirt beyond the target, and the third nicked the edge of the container, rocking it.

"Better," Slocum said. "You'll improve with practice." He couldn't suppress a grin. "In the meantime, if you meet a gent named Clay Allison or Wild Bill Hickok, just offer to buy them a drink. Reload and try again."

The sun had dropped almost to the horizon before Slocum finally called a halt. Link had fired more than thirty rounds, with six hits and a dozen others that would have been close enough if the can had been a man's chest. Slocum held out his palm. "Let me see that Colt," he said.

Link handed the weapon to Slocum. There were still two rounds in the cylinder. Slocum hefted the gun, tested its balance, then swept the muzzle up and fired twice. Dirt kicked at the base of the can on his first shot; the second slug knocked the can spinning.

"Too stiff in the action, and the front sight's too high. We can fix that easy enough, Link. Once it's tuned up, you'll do better." Slocum lifted his own Peacemaker from its holster and handed it to Link. "Try this one. I think you'll be able to tell the difference."

Link lifted the weapon, paused for a second, and squeezed the trigger. His eyes went wide as the can spun high in the air. "God," Link said, "I hardly touched that trigger."

Slocum held out his hand. "I'll fix yours so it has less of a hair trigger." He took the .44-40, ejected the spent round, and thumbed a fresh cartridge into place. "By the way," Slocum said, "I don't loan my gun to just anybody."

Link shook his head in wonder. "Thanks, Slocum. Lord, I never picked up such a fine piece of work in my life."

Slocum grinned at the youngster. "A man's only as good as his tools, Link," he said. "Let's go sharpen yours up a bit."

The two strode back to their camp on the far side of the seep. Link knelt beside his saddle.

"Slocum?"

"Yes?"

Link shucked the Winchester .45-90 from its saddle boot. "Maybe I'm a lost cause with a Colt, but honestly, I *can* shoot a rifle." He lifted the weapon, settled the crescent-shaped brass buttplate into his shoulder, and drew a quick bead.

Slocum turned just in time to see one of the target cans bounce high in the air as the thunderous muzzle blast of the big-bore rifle jarred against his ears. The range had been almost two hundred yards, the target small, and even Slocum's keen eyesight had trouble picking it up against the twilight. He pursed his lips in a silent whistle.

"Link," he said, "you can sure as hell handle a long gun. That's a good thing to know about the man you're riding with."

Link nodded at the compliment, racked a fresh round into the Winchester, and knelt to pick up the spent brass. He dropped the empty cartridge into a shirt pocket. "Always save the brass," he said offhandedly. "I load my own for this weapon. I finally came up with a recipe the rifle digests well."

"Like deep-dish apple pie, judging from that shot," Slocum said. "Now, if you'll gather up a bit of firewood, we'll have some supper and see if we can't take the rough edges off that new Colt of yours."

Link strode into the scraggly brush at the edge of camp and returned a few minutes later with a double armload of sticks, small branches, and a few chunks of driftwood. Slocum watched as Link piled the wood over the blackened circle used by Preacher Whiteside's gang hours before. *The kid's so green he doesn't even know how to build a campfire,* Slocum thought in wry amusement.

"Link," Slocum said, "we're cooking bacon, beans, and coffee here, not frying a whole steer." He knelt beside the knee-high pile of wood. "When you're laying a fire, remember what the Indians say: 'Indians build small fire and sit close; white man builds big fire and stands way back.' I'll show you how it's done."

Slocum laid the fire Comanche-style, with the smaller twigs that would start the blaze in the center, a few larger limbs across them, and finally added four wrist-sized pieces of driftwood, each facing one of the four directions. He touched a lucifer to the kindling. Moments later a small blaze flickered and took hold.

Slocum glanced at Link. "A small fire doesn't make as much smoke," he said, "and it can't be seen from as far away as a big one. That's something to remember when you're on the trail of some nasty-tempered men with big guns."

Link nodded in understanding.

"As the bigger limbs here burn, all you have to do is push them into the fire to keep the blaze fed. It'll give plenty of heat to cook by without scorching your *cojones* in the process. Bring my pack and we'll have what you might call a tracker's banquet."

Full darkness had descended by the time Link and Slocum had eaten, then cleaned and stored the utensils. The coffeepot steamed at the edge of the small blaze.

Slocum rummaged in his pack, drew out a small bundle wrapped in canvas, and sat near the edge of the fire where the light was best. "Hand me that Colt, Link," he said. Slocum noted with satisfaction that Link took the time to unload the gun first. He unwrapped the bundle and spread his tools—a penknife with the point filed to the shape of a screwdriver, a miniature blacksmith's metal punch, and a chunk of whetstone barely the size of his thumb.

Link edged closer as Slocum stripped the .45 and placed the pieces in careful order. He ran his fingertips over the trigger and sear mechanisms and handed the parts to Link. "Feel anything?"

Link ran a thumb over the sear, his brow wrinkled in concentration. "Rough spot here," he said. "Feels like a machine burr of some sort."

"Colonel Colt makes a good weapon, but I've never seen a perfect one yet." Slocum reached for the parts. "We'll hone the burr off, then cut down the sear a bit. That'll give you a lighter and smoother trigger pull." Slocum picked up the whetstone. "Meantime, you clean the rest of the gun. Black powder residue can clog a Colt quicker than a man would think."

Link picked up the receiver and barrel assembly, then reached for his rifle.

Slocum raised an eyebrow. "What are you going to do with the long gun?"

"Why, clean it, of course."

"Slocum's Rule Number Four, Link: Never strip all your weapons at the same time. You never know when you're going to need a gun, and they don't shoot worth a damn when they're in pieces. Clean the pistol first. When it's finished and reloaded, then you can clean the rifle."

Link shook his head in dismay. "God, Slocum, you must think I'm a complete fool."

Slocum grinned at Link. "No, I don't. You're just in a different element. Nobody is born knowing everything. You're learning, Link. It takes time."

Slocum fell silent, concentrating on his work. Thirty minutes later Link's Colt was tuned, oiled, and reassembled. Slocum handed the weapon to the youngster. "Dry fire it a few times and see if that doesn't feel better," he said.

Link pointed the weapon away from the fire, thumbed the hammer, and squeezed the trigger, then turned to Slocum. "Smooth as silk," he said. "It feels like a different gun. Maybe I can shoot a little straighter now. Slocum, you should have been a gunsmith."

Slocum shrugged. "A trade like that ties a man down. I just take care of my tools." He nodded toward Link's Winchester. "Reload the Colt, clean the rifle, and it'll be time to turn in. We've got a long ride ahead tomorrow. I want to be on the trail at first light."

Later, Slocum lay on his back, a couple of shots of whiskey warm in his belly, a cigarillo in his fingers, and stared at the blanket of stars in the black sky above. In the distance a coyote yipped and wailed; an answering howl came from beyond the seep. An owl glided overhead, hunting on silent wings, and the soft whistling call of a night bird sounded from the thicket. *This is what life should be all about,* he thought, *and it could be, if it wasn't for people like Preacher Whiteside.*

"Slocum?"

"Yes?"

"Can I ask something that's none of my business?"

"Go ahead," Slocum said. "There's no rule that says I have to answer if I don't want to."

"How did you wind up out here?"

Slocum sighed. The question took the scabs off a few old sores. "The war, sort of," he said. "After it was over. I went back to the family farm in Calhoun County, Georgia. I was sick of all the killing by then. I thought I'd put it behind me, that I'd never have to touch a gun again. It didn't work out. A carpetbagger judge tried to steal the farm. Claimed the taxes on the property hadn't been paid. He came back a few days later with another man, a hired gun. I killed them both, burned the house and barn to the ground, and headed west. I've been drifting ever since. It's not a bad life, most of the time."

"Are you still wanted in Georgia?"

Slocum took a drag from the cigarillo and exhaled the rich smoke though his nostrils. "Maybe, maybe not. Why? Are you planning to take me in, hoping for a reward?"

Link grinned and shook his head. "I may be young and green, Slocum, but I'm no damn fool." He fell silent for a moment, staring at the stars. "Slocum, how many men have you killed?"

"More than I like to think about," Slocum said softly, "but, except for during the war, only those who deserved it or who forced my hand."

"What's it like? To kill a man, I mean."

Slocum took a long drag from the cigarillo and stared for a moment in silence at the glowing end of the tube of tobacco. "It depends on the circumstances and the man," he finally said. "Some, you regret. Others, there's no bad feeling. It's like stomping a rattler who's about to bite you or someone else. In the war, it was just a job. That bothered me some, because I didn't know the men. All I knew was that they wore the wrong uniform." He paused and studied the stars overhead for a moment. "I wondered sometimes if they had wives, mothers, or families back home. But the army kept me too busy to think about it much. Speaking of which, I don't much care to think about it now." He snuffed the spent cigarillo in the dirt at his side, then buried it beneath the sand. "What about you, Link? What brought you out here?"

Link sighed. "Boredom with the big city, I suppose. I'd read everything I could get my hands on about the West. It sounded like a good place to be. So I just packed up and came on."

"It is a good place to be, Link. On the frontier it's not where a man has been or what he's done in the past that's important. It's who he is and what he's doing now that counts." Slocum settled back onto his bedroll. "How did your folks take to the idea of your coming West?"

Slocum heard Link's wry chuckle. "Dad raised hell. He wanted me to go into the family mercantile business. But there wasn't much there for me. I have an older brother. The business will be his when Dad retires. I would have been just another hired hand. I wanted to make a name for myself on my own merits. Mom was on my side. I could tell she was hurt that I would leave home, but she's an independent sort herself. She understood."

The two men fell silent for several minutes, listening to the cry of coyotes and the rustle of small animals as the night creatures went about their business of living in the brush and tall grass around the camp.

It was Link who finally broke the silence.

"Slocum, I've never killed a man. All the glamour went out of the idea that night in the saloon when I was looking down the barrel of that Colt in your hand. But if those bastards out there have—" he paused for a moment, as if groping for the right words, "—if they've harmed Victoria, I don't think I'll have any fits of remorse over dropping a hammer on them."

Slocum squirmed between his blankets, wallowed a depression in the sand for his hips to rest in, and sighed. "Keep that thought in mind, Link," he said, "because when the time comes, you'll shoot—or all three of us will be dead. Now, get some sleep. It's going to be a long day tomorrow."

5

Victoria Tucker clung to the mane of the borrowed pack horse, trying to keep her balance as they descended the steep canyon wall to the Cimarron River below.

The Cimarron Strip was a gash of badlands in the area known as No Man's Land, a narrow strip of rugged canyons slashing through the nearly flat plains north of the Texas Panhandle, south of Colorado and Kansas and west of the Indian Territory.

Victoria had heard of the Strip, and the stories were not reassuring. It was an area beyond the reach of the law, beyond the jurisdiction of even those few lawmen with the courage to enter the badlands. It was said that only three types of men were to be found in the Strip: those who were on the dodge, those who were dead, and those who soon would be dead.

Her heart skidded into her belly as her mount stumbled on the narrow slope and almost went down; the unexpected motion threw her forward against the rough wood frame of the pack saddle. She felt a sharp sting in her left thigh as loose shale and stones clattered down the fifty-foot drop to the canyon floor below. Victoria strained to regain her seat and lifted the reins to help the horse get its head back up and its feet beneath it. The horse finally regained its footing, blew its surge of fear away with a flutter of nostrils, and dropped its head to study the trail.

The single-file column of riders straggled to a halt at the bottom of the steep grade. Preacher Whiteside raised a hand. Dirk Campbell, the half-breed with the smoke-colored eyes, trotted up to the outlaw leader, his scout of the river completed.

"Couple of cowboys camped up ahead a mile or so in a stand of cottonwoods," Campbell said. "Looks like they're hunting strays. Got a dozen head of cattle and four horses wearing the Rocking T brand."

"Did they see you?"

Campbell shook his head.

"Good," Preacher said. He reined his horse around to face the others in the outlaw band. "As you see, the Lord provides for His servants. He has delivered unto us fresh mounts and bread with which to continue our work in His name." He pointed a bony finger at Clell Bates. "Clell, stay with Jubal. The Almighty has spared him this long; there must be a grand purpose for that."

Victoria glanced at the wounded man. Jubal still slumped over the saddle horn, his face pale and features twisted in agony. *A normal man would have died two days ago,* she thought.

"Fowler, it is time you joined in shedding the blood of the Philistines. You will take the right flank. Jeb, you take the left. Dirk will join you on the field of battle." He waved a hand toward the half-breed. "Lead the way, my son. Take us to these mortal sinners. And you, child," he said with a twisted grin at Victoria, "shall ride with me into the enemy camp. They will perceive no danger from a man riding with a young woman."

Victoria started to protest, but checked the impulse.

"You will not cry out a warning." Preacher's voice took on a menacing tone. "If you do, I will have no choice but to kill you—or, perhaps, leave your fate in the hands of the other members of my flock."

A chill traced icy fingers down Victoria's spine. She was painfully aware of Jeb Dawson's gaze, the hate showing through the clotted blood from the cuts on his bruised face. She knew that two more innocent men were about to die. And there was absolutely nothing she could do to stop it.

Preacher grunted in obvious satisfaction. "Wait for my signal, soldiers, then open fire. Now, come, my friends. Let us go gather this manna from heaven." The half-breed reined his horse about and kneed the animal into a trot upriver. Preacher waved Victoria forward. "Come, child. Ride at my side."

Victoria did as she was told.

The mile ride to the stand of cottonwoods seemed an eternity to Victoria. The reins turned slick from the cold sweat of her palms and the pain from the splinter still in her thigh after the near-fall throbbed with each beat of her racing heart. Then they reached the edge of the camp.

Two young men in range garb stood by a small fire, each with a rifle in hand, and stared warily as Preacher and Victoria rode into the clearing. Beyond the screen of cottonwoods and underbrush, Victoria heard the lowing of a small herd of cattle and the snorts and snuffles of horses.

Preacher raised a hand in greeting.

"Ah," Preacher said, "some fellow travelers along life's stony path. And a welcome sight indeed for my daughter and I. May we share your fire? We have a few meager rations— and yon coffeepot emits a tempting aroma."

Indecision flickered for a moment on the two young men's clean-shaven faces. Then the sandy-haired one nearest the fire smiled and lowered his rifle. "Light and set, folks. Sorry about pointing these rifles at you, but a man never knows who might ride up on him out here."

The second rider hesitated, then finally lowered his own rifle. Preacher dismounted and nodded for Victoria to do the same. He tied the horses to a low cottonwood limb, pulled two tin cups from his pack, and strode toward the fire. "A blessing it is to find company on a long and arduous journey. I am the Reverend Whiteside, traveler in this wasteland, bringing the word to those who have no church at hand. This young lady—" he waved a hand toward Victoria "—is my beloved daughter. Are you gentlemen of the Christian faith?"

The sandy-haired cowboy grinned. "Well, Reverend, you might say I'm a believer. We could use a prayer or two to help us round up this drift stock." He leaned his rifle against the swell of a worn stock saddle and reached for the coffeepot.

Preacher squatted beside the fire and waited as the young cowboy filled the two cups. Preacher sipped at the thick, hot brew and sighed. "The purest of nectars, my son. You make a fine cup of coffee."

Victoria noted that Preacher kept a close eye on the second cowboy, a slim, black-haired man. He still carried his rifle and wore a suspicious expression. Her stomach churned in dread; she fought back the powerful urge to cry out a warning. Logic told her it would serve no purpose except to get herself killed along with the two riders.

"May I recite some passages from the Good Book to ease your travails, my friends?" Preacher reached inside his frock coat and brought out a battered Bible.

"That won't be necessary, Reverend," the sandy-haired one said with a grin. "I can quote most of it to you, anyway—chapter and verse."

"Ah, then. You know the Book of Revelations?"

"By heart."

Preacher casually put the book at his side. He left his hand on the Bible, near the butt of his holstered Colt. "'And I looked, and beheld a light horse.'"

"A pale horse, sir," the cowboy said, "'and his name that sat on him was Death.'"

"Very good, son," Preacher said. "I am he who sat upon that pale horse." The thin man dropped his coffee cup, swept the pistol from its holster, and fired. The impact of the heavy slug tumbled the young man onto his back. The second cowboy yelped in surprise and swung his rifle toward Preacher. The whipcrack of two rifle shots rattled through the clearing. The dark-haired cowboy staggered, spun, and fell. Blood spurted from his neck and a second stain spread over his back. Preacher stood, strode to the bodies, and shot each man once more in the head.

Victoria sat in stunned silence at the sudden violence, her mouth working but forming no sounds, her ears ringing from the muzzle blasts. For a split second, she thought about making a sprint toward the underbrush, to escape while the outlaws were distracted. Almost as quickly, she abandoned the thought. There was nowhere to run that they wouldn't track her down.

The half-breed was the first to stride from the cover of the trees. Smoke wisped from the muzzle of his rifle. Jeb Dawson emerged from the far side of the clearing, thumbing a fresh round into the loading port of his Winchester. A moment later Dade Fowler appeared, his face pale.

"Dirk, gather their weapons, strip the bodies, and distribute the guns and clothing among our warriors. Dade, you and Jeb fetch your horses," Preacher said. Excitement danced in the pale blue eyes. "Get ropes on the feet of these sinners and drag the offal from our camp. Don't bother to bury them. Their flesh shall feed the buzzards and jackals of the night." He ejected the spent cartridges, reloaded, and holstered his Colt. "And check on our new mounts. Make sure they haven't bolted and that their tethers are secure."

Victoria blinked back tears of outrage and horror as Preacher turned to her. "You see, child? The Lord provides for His messengers." He cackled in sudden glee. "With a little help from Colonel Colt and Major Winchester, of course." The laugh ended as quickly as it came. "Check their supplies, girl. We be in need of coffee, bacon, beans, sugar, and salt to restore our diminished larder. Move quickly, now."

Victoria hurried to the packs beyond the campfire. Maybe, she thought, one of the men had a spare weapon—a pistol or at least a hunting knife—stored in the packs. She tried to ignore the naked, blood-soaked bodies on the ground, tried not to watch as Dade and Jeb, now mounted, flicked loops toward the feet of the downed men. Preacher snubbed the ropes tight around the ankles of the corpses. The bodies lurched, arms dragging outstretched in the sandy soil, as the two horsemen spurred their mounts toward the trees beyond.

The dead men's packs held a sack of flour, one of sugar, another of coffee, a slab of bacon, canned goods, blankets, two unopened bottles of whiskey—but no weapons. Not even a knife. Victoria's shoulders slumped in dejection. Then her fingers closed around a small box that had settled into a corner of one pack. She slipped the cardboard container from the pouch and glanced at the label. It read *Remington .22 Rimfire Short*. She cautiously shook the box. Only a slight rattle sounded; if it contained ammunition, there wasn't much. Still, her spirits lifted as she shielded the box and carefully pried open an end flap. There were eight small cartridges inside. Where there was ammunition there should be a gun. A man wouldn't carry shells unless he had a weapon to fit. She glanced over her shoulder at the men by the campfire. No one was watching at the moment. She rummaged again, quickly, through the pile of supplies. There was no weapon. *It must be somewhere else,* she thought. *Maybe I'll get lucky and find it before they do.* She opened the cartridge box once more, dumped the small shells into her palm, and slipped them into the pocket of her Levi's. She held the empty box for a moment, her mind racing. If one of the men found the box, they would assume, as she had, that there would be a weapon around someplace. She flattened the box and slipped it inside her waistband. She winced, startled, at the crunch of boots on the sand behind her.

"Anything usable here, child?"

Victoria swallowed against the sudden tightness in her throat, the fear of discovery blended with shock and a feeling of dread. "Yes, sir. Food, mostly."

"Good, good." Preacher's tone was that of a satisfied, even smug, man. He had just murdered two men in cold blood, and he seemed quite pleased with himself. Preacher surveyed the supplies spread beside the packs. "The Lord's bounty has fallen upon us again. If we proceed with care, this will be sufficient to see us into New Mexico." He reached out a bony hand, plucked one of the whiskey bottles from amid the booty, then motioned to Victoria. "Come, child. You will help prepare our feast of thanksgiving this night." He strode to a cottonwood tree, leaned against the trunk, and twisted the cork from the whiskey bottle.

Moments later, Dade Fowler rode back into the clearing. His rope was once again tied to the saddle with a thin leather thong looped around the horn. He dismounted, tied his horse to a nearby tree, and walked to her side.

"Are you all right, Victoria?"

"I'm—a little shaken," Victoria said, aware of the quaver in her voice. "Those poor men! Why couldn't he have just taken their property and set them afoot, Dade? Why did he have to kill them like that?"

Dade glanced at the tall man standing by the tree and half-shrugged. "It's his way, Victoria. That's what makes him so dangerous. I'm sorry you had to see that."

Victoria lifted her head to gaze into Dade Fowler's eyes. "It hurt almost as much to know you helped kill them," she said.

Dade shook his head, glanced around to make sure no one would overhear, and then lowered his voice to a whisper. "For what it's worth, I didn't, Victoria. Maybe I didn't try to stop it, but I never fired my rifle. It's one thing to kill a man in a fair fight. It's another to bushwhack a stranger for nothing more than a few dollars' worth of supplies."

Victoria forced a smile. "I'm glad to know that, Dade. I've known from the first that you aren't like the rest of these animals. I'm glad you're here. I—I'm counting on you to protect me, Dade. To keep those awful men from doing something terrible to me." She reached out, put a hand on the wiry muscles of his forearm, and let her voice drop low and husky. "I could make it worth your while to help me. With money—or anything else you want."

Victoria knew she was pushing her luck with the young outlaw. But at the moment he was all she had. Dade was the only one of this group who seemed to have a sense of decency and honor. She felt no remorse at trying to use him to her own ends. For a moment Victoria thought Dade was about to speak as his gaze darted about the camp. Then he abruptly pulled his arm free of her grip and strode away. Victoria felt a presence at the edge of the clearing, turned, and found herself staring into the face of Clell Bates a few yards away. Bates seemed amused. He held the man called Jubal in the saddle. Jubal's clothing was soaked with sweat, his eyes closed, teeth clenched against pain and a raging fever.

Bates did not speak, but he stared for a moment at Victoria before reining his horse closer to the campsite. He pulled up, dismounted, and helped the wounded man from the saddle. Victoria felt her chest tighten as Bates whispered something to Preacher Whiteside. Preacher glanced toward Victoria, then toward the retreating figure of Dade Fowler. Finally, he shrugged, muttered something, and strode toward the campfire.

"Come, gentlemen," Preacher called, his tone cheerful. He lifted the hand holding the whiskey bottle aloft. "Let us take our communion and give thanks for deliverance." He downed a hefty swallow and sighed. "It is not the blood of Christ, but it will suffice." He offered the bottle to the half-breed. "Join us, Dirk, in our communion."

The breed hesitated, then lifted the bottle, took a small sip, winced, and started to hand it back. Jeb Dawson grabbed the bottle from his hand. "Never heard of a damn Injun who didn't know how to drink," he said, sarcasm thick on his tongue.

Dirk Campbell glared at Dawson. Anger flickered in the deep gray eyes, the first outward show of emotion Victoria had seen in the man. Then the breed shrugged, apparently choosing to ignore the insult. Victoria noted the tension between the two gunmen. It was one more thing she might exploit if and when the opportunity came.

"Dirk," Preacher said, "ride upriver about a mile. You'll find a canyon that opens off to the south. A magnificent work of the Creator, studded with trees and a fine, pure spring. At the head of the canyon is a small rock cabin. There you will find a Mexican. He is called Ortega, and he is almost as good a doctor as he is a horse thief. A man doubly blessed, you might say. Bring him to tend our wounded."

Dirk nodded and strode toward his horse. Moments later the sound of hoofbeats moving out at a quick trot sounded beyond the clearing.

Preacher sat cross-legged beside the fire, the bottle between his knees, and poked through the supplies taken from the dead men. He glanced up at Victoria and smiled. "Well, child," he said, "you will benefit as well from the bounty delivered here today. You will have your own bed—" he waved a hand toward a roll covered by a groundsheet— "and your own saddle, and I believe the boots and hat of the smaller man will fit you. That should make your travels with us more comfortable."

Victoria nodded. The thought of sleeping in the blankets of a dead man, and riding in his saddle, brought an inward shudder of unease. The feeling passed, pushed aside by a silent sigh of relief. At least she would no longer have to lie on Preacher's blankets. One day, she feared, his revulsion for female flesh might pass. Maybe the distance between their bedrolls would delay that time. And with a proper saddle, she might have a better chance at escape.

Jeb Dawson, his battered face already flushed by the effects of whiskey, sat across from Victoria. His gaze bored into her. "The little bitch can share my bed anytime, Preacher," he said. Dawson was staring at her chest. Victoria became aware that the cloth of the borrowed shirt did little to cover her breasts. She hunched her shoulders forward in an effort to ease the push of nipples against the cloth.

Preacher glared at Dawson. A muscle in his jaw twitched. "I'll have no such talk in my camp, Jeb Dawson." His voice was cold and hard. "No man is to violate the virgin of Babylon. Or have you forgotten the message I have already delivered to you?"

Dawson shifted his gaze to Whiteside. The hate in the pistol-whipped outlaw's eyes flared brighter. "Damn you, Whiteside, I'll make you pay for that!" His hand drifted toward the butt of the pistol at his waist.

Preacher's eyes narrowed until they were little more than slits. "Remember your place, Dawson. And bear in mind the wisdom of Solomon: 'They who be punished in the sight of men yet hope for immortality.' You have been punished for your transgression. Touch the pistol and you will forfeit all hope of immortality on this earth."

Dawson stared at the thin man for several heartbeats. "I've half a mind to take you on, Preacher."

"You flatter yourself, Jeb, for you've not half a mind at all," Whiteside said, his voice flat and without emotion. "But if you choose to lose the other half, make your play."

Jeb Dawson's muscles tensed; for a moment Victoria thought the stocky man was actually going to go for the pistol. Then fear pushed aside the murderous gleam in Dawson's eyes. His shoulders slumped and his hand fell away from the gun. "Aw, hell, Preacher," he said, "I reckon it was just the whiskey talkin'. I'm smarter than to draw down on you. I seen you work a Colt before."

"Are you apologizing, Jeb?"

Dawson's jaw muscles twitched, but he nodded. "I reckon so." The admission brought a fresh wave of color to the already flushed face.

"Accepted. Even a soldier of the Lord is not above mistakes. Don't let it happen again."

Dawson climbed unsteadily to his feet. "You're the boss, Preacher." He turned his head to glare at Victoria. "But there's one thing you're dead wrong about. If missy here is a virgin, I'm a damned pack mule."

Preacher chuckled softly. "Then quiet your spirit, friend Jeb, and remember that the ass who brays too loudly may lose a portion of his own ass." The thin man's grin faded as quickly as it came. "Keep your hands from her, Dawson, or I will kill you next time. Her mission is not the carnal satisfaction of men, but the deliverance of them to safety beyond the Jordan. Or in our particular case, the Rio Grande. At the moment, they are one and the same."

The confrontation ended at the sound of a hail from the western side of the camp. Moments later Dirk Campbell rode in, followed by a small, hunched Mexican on a mouse-colored mustang. Preacher came to his feet. "Ah, my good friend Ortega. Welcome to my humble camp."

The hunched Mexican dismounted and took the Preacher's hand, a broad smile spread over a wrinkled and toothless face. "Reverend, it is a treat to see you again. I understand you have need of my humble talents? Let us attend that first, and later renew acquaintance."

Preacher draped a long arm over Ortega's bony shoulders and led him to the blankets where Jubal lay, barely conscious and moaning in misery. Ortega stripped the cloth away from the shoulder wound, grunted in satisfaction, and waved a hand in a circular motion. Clell Bates knelt by Jubal and rolled the injured man onto his belly. Ortega lifted Jubal's shirt, examined the kidney wound, then stood and shook his head.

"I am sorry," he said. "The wound in the lower back is beyond my limited ability as a healer." He stood for a moment, staring down at the moaning Jubal. "By Mary and Joseph, he should have died long ago. The wound is inflamed, ringed with what we call the proud flesh. The infection will spread as the locusts."

"Is there naught you can do for him, friend?"

Ortega shrugged. "Nothing. If he lives until you reach a town with a real doctor who has real medicine, he might have a chance. I would not wager my horse on it even then."

Preacher sighed and shrugged his thin shoulders. "So be it. His fate remains in the hands of God. Come, my friend Ortega. Share our supper, have a drink, and I will pay you for your time and trouble."

The meal passed without further incident. The men ate in silence except for Preacher and the wiry Mexican, who traded tales of past exploits in a strange mixture of Spanish—which Victoria did not understand—and English, with what seemed to be an Indian word tossed in on occasion.

Victoria ate her own supper in silence, hardly tasting the food. In the near distance a coyote yelped, greeting the sunset. The sound sent a quiver through Victoria. The coyote, or others like him, would have their own supper after nightfall. The flesh of two innocent men.

Finally, Ortega handed his plate to Victoria, took a final sip of whiskey, and stood. "I must be on my way, friend Whiteside," he said. "God go with you."

"Come, Ortega, and ride with us. We can use a good man, as it seems we are to lose one of our own."

"Your offer is tempting," Ortega said solemnly, "but I must remain here on the river. There are many fine horses yet to be stolen."

Preacher chuckled in admiration. "Good hunting, Ortega."

The wiry little Mexican touched fingers to his sombrero in salute and strode from the clearing.

Preacher took another slug from the nearly empty bottle in his fist, then turned to Victoria. "When you have finished your camp chores, child, spread yon blankets—" he nodded toward one of the dead men's bedrolls "—at my side. The morning will come soon, and with it we ride."

Victoria turned to cleaning up the dishes from the meal. Back home it was a chore she hated and dreaded. Out here it was a diversion, something to keep her hands occupied.

Several times as she worked, she felt the pressure of Jeb Dawson's gaze. She tried to ignore the man. *Lord, please,* she prayed as she worked, *if it has to be, let it be anyone but that animal.*

The sun had dropped from sight before Victoria finished her chores. A curious twilight settled over the clearing, one which seemed to leave no shadows and bathed everything in a pinkish-gold light, the color of tintypes on display at the bank back home. The spooky cast of the atmosphere did nothing to soothe her already frayed nerves. The coyote yapped again, nearer this time. The creature probably was stalking the bodies outside the camp, Victoria thought.

She stood, strode to the pile of supplies taken from the dead men, and lifted what seemed to be the cleaner of the two bedrolls. She strode slowly back to the fire, knelt, and untied the rawhide strips wrapped around the bedroll. There seemed to a small lump at one end. She cautiously reached inside. The lump yielded the cool touch of metal and wood worn smooth. Her fingers traced the outline of a small pistol. Victoria felt her heartbeat quicken. She glanced around, trying to make her movements casual. Preacher was watching her. If he caught her trying to conceal a weapon—

"Preacher?" Clell Bates's voice rumbled from the edge of the camp.

"Yes?" The tall man turned toward Bates. Victoria knew it might be her only chance; she grabbed the barrel of the pistol, jammed it against her belly, and bent to unroll the blankets. Then she thrust the little pistol beneath the top fold of the canvas groundsheet.

"The way I reckon it," Bates said, "it's about time to divvy up what we've got coming. If it's all right with you," he added hastily.

Preacher sighed. "Not yet, friend Clell," he said. "It is but a short ride into the small town called Chicota in New Mexico. You will be given enough coin to satisfy your needs of the flesh. We will not divide the complete spoils of war until we have crossed the Rio Grande."

Victoria breathed a sigh of relief. The distraction had been enough for her to conceal the pistol. The sense of relief turned to a sudden, cold surge of fear as she felt eyes on her. She glanced toward the edge of the camp. The half-breed was watching her, his eyes without expression in the growing gloom. Her breath caught in her throat as she waited, not knowing if the man called Dirk had seen her store the weapon, or if he would sound the alarm.

Dirk slowly turned his head away. He gave no outward indication that he had seen anything. *Stay calm, Victoria,* she told herself. *If he didn't notice, you're all right; if he did, there's nothing to be done about it now.*

Victoria sat at the edge of the bedroll, unlaced and removed her shoes, and slipped between the coarse blankets. They held a strong odor of horse sweat and a fainter but still distinct smell of man. The scent of a dead man. Her fingers probed her thigh, found the splinter from the wood fork of the pack, and pulled it free. She winced at the quick stab of pain. It passed quickly. She waited, willing herself to have patience, until the others in the camp began to settle in for the night.

She started at an unexpected touch on her shoulder. Preacher stood above her, his hawklike nose in silhouette against the dying fire. Preacher had a length of rope in his hand.

"Hold out your arm, child," the outlaw said.

Victoria did as she was told. She felt the coarse bite of the rope around her wrist as Preacher tugged it snug and tied it with a knot of some type she had never seen. Preacher payed out the thin rope until he reached his own bedroll, then looped the tether about his own wrist.

"Now," he said, "it will not be necessary to have a sentry stand watch over you, child." His tone turned hard despite the slight smile on the stubbled face. "Attempt to remove the rope and it will not go well for you," he said. Victoria nodded her understanding.

It seemed to Victoria that an eternity passed before the snores of the outlaws began to saw into the quiet of the camp. Still she waited until, finally, she felt safe enough to slip her free hand down to the small pistol.

Victoria desperately wished she had paid more attention to firearms. She had been around them all her life, but the feel of the pistol was completely foreign to her hand. She couldn't even tell by feel if it was loaded, and she dared not risk pulling it out to examine the gun visually. But the cold steel and tiny wooden grip were somehow reassuring to the touch. At least now she had something, even if she wasn't sure how to use it.

A sharp edge of folded cardboard gouged against her belly. The cartridge box. She knew she had to get rid of it before it was discovered. She eased the flattened container from beneath her waistband, carefully clawed a small depression in the sand by the edge of her bedroll, and put the box in the shallow hole. She scooped sand over it with her free hand. With luck, no one would find it tomorrow.

The faint westerly breeze brought a chill to Victoria's belly. The wind carried the faint, distant sound of predators snapping and growling as they quarreled over the remains of the two men. She tried to shake from her mind the image of coyotes tearing at the dead flesh. The scene would not be banished. Victoria knew that she would get no sleep that night.

Slocum came awake with a start, his hand clamped around the butt of the Peacemaker at his side. The sound that tore him back to consciousness was that of a pistol being drawn to full cock.

Then he sighed and half-smiled. He should have grown accustomed by now to the racket Link made each morning and evening, and in every spare moment on the trail. The kid was practicing again. Slocum watched in the pale, ghostly light of the false dawn as the young man stood twenty yards from camp, pistol in hand. Link dropped the weapon back into its holster, flexed his shoulders, and drew.

Slocum shook his head. The kid was improving with practice, but he was still slow as a Missouri plow mule.

"Relax, Link!" Slocum called out. He saw the young man flinch, startled at the unexpected sound. "Don't fight the weapon! Flow with it. Think smooth!"

Slocum kicked back the canvas groundsheet that covered his blankets, drew in a deep breath of the chill predawn air, and reached for a cigarillo. *Might as well get up and on with it,* he thought. He fired the smoke, rose, and built a small fire for coffee and breakfast. Slocum kept a close eye on Link as he went about his morning camp chores. *By God, he is getting better. There may be some hope for the kid yet,* Slocum mused. The quick reflexes of youth smoothed out a few of the rough edges of inexperience. *He'll probably just get us all killed, but I'll give him credit for one thing. He's trying.* "Link," he called, "let the Colt rest a bit. Coffee'll be ready in a few minutes. Tend the horses. We'll be moving out at first full light."

Link dropped the Colt back into its holster and strode toward camp. Slocum stood on the west side of the small fire, nostrils flared as he smelled the breeze and stared toward the horizon.

"Problem, Slocum?" Link asked.

"Maybe. I think we've got a storm building."

Link gazed toward the western horizon, a black smudge against the pale wash of light from a sun as yet unseen. "Don't see any clouds," he said.

"They're coming," Slocum said. "Smell the air, Link."

Link sniffed.

"What do you smell?"

Link shook his head. "Nothing."

"That's it, son," Slocum said. "There should be the scent of dust in the air. It smells clean, and out here that usually means rain." Slocum turned and waved toward the horses. The animals stood alert, their own nostrils flared. All faced the west, ears pointed toward the horizon. "They smell it, too," Slocum said. He squatted beside the fire. "Horses are good weather forecasters," he said. "Besides that, my shoulder's a little stiff this morning. Old bullet hole tightens up when a change in the weather is on the way. We'd best get a move on, Link. We don't want to be caught in open country like this when the storm breaks. Saddle up while I throw a few slices of bacon in the skillet. No telling when we may get a chance to eat again. On the trail you eat when you can, sleep when you can, and try to stay alive the rest of the time."

Link shook his head. "Not a cloud in the sky and you see a storm coming, Slocum. I think this time, all that trail sense you've been talking about is dead wrong."

"Silver dollar says we get wet before sundown," Slocum said. "If we're going to gain any ground on Whiteside, we'd best do it early in the day. Now, get cracking with those horses."

They were in the saddle less than an hour later. Slocum's gaze constantly swept the rolling prairie, with an occasional glance at the grass beneath. The outlaw band's tracks followed an almost arrow-straight line. By noon, Slocum calculated, he and Link would be in the Cimarron Strip; by midafternoon at the Cimarron River itself.

Link, riding at Slocum's right, was still practicing his draw. "Slocum?"

"Yes?"

"Is it hard to shoot from horseback?"

Slocum stifled a wry grin. "Hard enough."

"I've read about people who can shoot an Indian off his horse when both of them are in a dead run. Seems like that might be something worth learning."

"Be my guest," Slocum said. "Next time we jump a jackrabbit on your side, let her rip."

Ulysses Grant Abraham Lincoln flashed a quick grin. Slocum saw the eagerness in Link's eyes and understood. A man could stand just so much practice until he had to test his hand.

They had traveled less than a half mile when Slocum spotted the gray form huddled beneath a stunted greasewood bush ahead. "Here's your rabbit up ahead, Link. Remember, if you kill it, you clean it."

Slocum took up the slack in the reins and let his horse drop a few paces back of Link's mount. Link rode with his hand on the butt of the pistol, shoulders hunched forward in anticipation.

The jackrabbit sprang from the brush. Link's pistol whipped up. A split second after the blast of the heavy Colt sounded, Link's black gelding flung its head to the left, bogged its ears between its front legs and fell apart, bucking, squealing, and breaking wind. Link stayed in the saddle for two jumps, lost a stirrup on the third, and his seat on the fourth. He sailed high into the air and landed with a heavy thump on his back.

Slocum trotted his mount to the downed man. Link sat up, a bewildered expression on his face.

"You all right, Link?"

Link finally managed to gasp air back into his lungs. He nodded. "I think so." His voice was a harsh, raspy croak.

"Keep your seat," Slocum said with a chuckle. "I'll fetch your horse."

Slocum caught up with the black within a half mile. The horse had stopped pitching and running and stood with its head cocked to one side. Slocum led the gelding back to where Link still sat. The youth's face was flushed in embarrassment beneath the dirt.

"Slocum, what got into that black, anyway?"

"About a half pound of powder smoke, for one thing," Slocum said. He made no attempt to keep the amused tone from his voice.

"But—I thought—"

"You didn't think, son. You assumed you could shoot a gun from that horse's back. Obviously, he isn't trained for it. And even if he was, you don't touch off a round right next to his ear. Horse doesn't like that much. They've got a way of letting you know when they don't like something."

A fresh flush of color flooded Link's cheeks. "Dammit, Slocum, why didn't you tell me that to start with?"

Slocum winked at the youngster. "Figured you'd learn it faster on your own. Man carrying a live bobcat by the hind leg learns how to do it a lot faster than if he had someone just tell him how."

Link stood and brushed the dirt from his clothing. The flush of anger and embarrassment faded. A slow grin began to spread across his dirt-smeared face. "You know, Slocum, a man could get killed with you as a teacher."

Slocum shrugged. "Maybe. First rule of shooting from horseback is don't do it unless you have to. Too hard to hit what you're shooting at. Second rule is that if you have to, turn your horse a bit to the side so the gun doesn't go off in his ear. That'll save you some hide in the short run."

Link took the reins, toed the stirrup, and mounted. The black's head was still cocked to one side; the horse shook its head as if to clear the ringing from its right ear. The black made no further attempt to pitch as Link settled into the saddle. Link glanced at Slocum. "You must think I'm a real idiot," he said.

Slocum chuckled. "Nope. Just green, but learning fast. And you passed the test."

Link looked puzzled. "What test?"

Slocum nodded toward the Colt Link had holstered. "You didn't lose your weapon."

Link glanced around. "Where's my rabbit?"

"About halfway to Wyoming by now, I'd guess."

"I missed?"

"By about three feet." Slocum touched knees to his mount. "Let's move out, Link. We've got a lot of ground to cover before the storm hits."

6

The first few drops of rain fell as Slocum and Link rode up
to the rim of a narrow, rugged canyon which fed the Cimarron
River two miles below.

The rain was little more than droplets of heavy mist, carried
on the gusty wind from towering thunderheads to the west.
Slocum checked his sorrel and studied the storm clouds with
a practiced eye.

Lightning flashed almost constantly among the high, twisting cloud mass. The cloud boiled and swirled within itself, torn
by the power of forces little understood by man. Beneath the
flat bottom of the seething mass, a smear of dark rain rode
the wind, swept into a graceful arc as it fell. A greenish cast
tinted the lower edge of the clouds and flashed a ghostly glow
as lightning sliced through the swirling mountain of white
and gray. Slocum was always a bit awed, watching the brute
force of nature build a locomotive that could run down most
anything in its path.

The raindrops that slapped against his hat brim grew fatter.
Where the land lay exposed, the drops hit the parched soil
and rolled into sand-covered balls. *This is going to be one
ring-tailed cat of a storm,* Slocum thought.

"I never saw a cloud that tall back East," Link said softly
at Slocum's side. "It's like God's mad about something."

"Everything's bigger, wilder, and meaner out here, Link,"

Slocum said. He studied the narrow game trail descending toward the canyon floor. "That storm's got hail in it. That's what makes the cloud green. I've seen men, horses, and cattle beaten to death by hailstones in some of these storms. We best find some cover before it gets here." He kneed his sorrel onto the steep trail. The pack horse snorted and sidestepped, nervous, but yielded to Slocum's sharp command and tug on the lead rope and fell into step behind the sorrel.

For the first few minutes, Slocum was too busy helping his horse keep its footing on the loose shale of the slope to worry about anything else. Finally the trail widened slightly and went into a sharp switchback a few yards below the lip of the canyon. Slocum turned in the saddle to check on Link. The young man sat hunched forward, body tense, both hands wrapped in a death grip on the saddle horn.

"Relax, Link!" Slocum called. "Lean back in the saddle and push against the stirrups with your feet! Help the horse; he knows what he's doing!"

The sorrel between Slocum's legs twitched as a lightning bolt ripped overhead. A sharp crack of thunder loud enough to hurt a man's ears rattled the canyon wall. The rain came harder; heavy, fat drops stung when they hit exposed skin, and the trail underfoot began to turn into a ribbon of slippery mud.

A thin stream of water already had begun to flow through the narrow canyon before Slocum reached the bottom of the steep slope. The rain came in sheets now; Slocum could barely see fifty feet ahead. But he felt, more than saw, the rocky outcrop on the west edge of the canyon, almost halfway up the side. He kneed the sorrel into a brisk trot.

The first hailstone, only the size of man's fingernail, bounced off the side of Slocum's leg just before he pulled his horse beneath the protection of the overhanging rock ledge. The overhang was large enough to protect two men and four horses from the hail. They wouldn't be dry, but at least they would be spared the main brunt of the storm. Slocum raised a hand in a signal to Link to stop, then stepped down and positioned his horses against the canyon wall. Link was close behind. The young man was soaked to the skin and shivered in the sudden blast of cold air that swept the canyon.

But, Slocum noted with satisfaction, Link took the time to make sure his horses were secure before worrying about his own comfort. The clatter of hail against soil and stone rose to a constant roar. Frozen chunks of ice grew larger, some almost as big as a man's fist. They struck with the force of a sledgehammer, bounced, and ricocheted away down the slope. Slocum ignored the clatter. The hailstones wouldn't reach them here unless the wind and storm changed directions abruptly. He lifted his Colt from his holster and checked the weapon. It was reasonably dry.

"Slocum?" Link had to shout to be heard over the crash of thunder and rattle of hailstones.

"Yes?"

"We passed a sort of cave a few yards below. Why didn't we stop there? It would have been better cover." Link brushed at the mist that drifted beneath the overhang and swirled like a heavy fog about the two men and their horses.

Slocum fished in his saddlebags for a dry cigarillo, cupped the cylinder of tobacco to protect it from the mist, scratched a lucifer into flame with a thumbnail, and fired the smoke. He waved a hand toward the cavelike hollow below. "Just keep an eye open, Link. You'll see."

For almost an hour the two men stood silent and watched a solid, blinding sheet of rain and ice slam into the canyon. Lightning cracked against the far canyon ridge. A barrage of thunder rolled almost constantly, one peal atop the last. Then the violent storm began to pass. The hail stopped. In the near distance another ominous rumble sounded above the receding growls of the storm.

Slocum pointed up the canyon. Link's eyes went wide in surprise and awe as a six-foot-high wall of water surged around a bend in the canyon, carrying sticks of driftwood, stunted trees, and other trash past the ledge where the two men stood. Within seconds, the top of Link's cave disappeared beneath the boiling, muddy onslaught.

"Flash flood," Slocum said. "If we'd stopped in the cave, we would have been dead by now."

"How did you know?"

Slocum gestured toward the far canyon wall, which had

become clearly visible again as the storm clouds passed. "What do you see over there, Link?"

Link squinted toward the rocks. "I don't see anything."

"Look again. See the line that runs along the canyon? A line of dead grass, sage, and pieces of driftwood?"

"Oh. I see it now."

"That's the high water mark of a canyon or arroyo, or any other place you might get ambushed by a flash flood. Stay above that line of trash and you'll be all right. Get below it in one of these storms and your body might wind up in the Gulf of Mexico. Something to keep in mind."

Link fell silent for a time. Sunlight brightened the canyon, fell on the dirty floodwaters below, and the big thunderstorm rumbled farther into the distance. "Slocum," Link finally said, "I would have stopped in that cave. I'm sure glad you didn't let me carry my own live bobcat this time."

Slocum grinned. "Little different situation here. Sometimes a man doesn't want to learn by pure experience." He glanced at the sky. "Storm's over. We'll move out as soon as the water goes down a bit. It will fall almost as fast as it rose."

Link plucked a small piece of shale from the canyon wall and scraped the stone against the mud on his boot soles. Then he glanced up, a frown on his face.

"Slocum, this storm will wipe out the trail. How are we going to find those bastards now?"

Slocum shrugged. "It'll slow us down some, maybe, but it's not that hard to find a bunch of men who have stolen money in their pockets." He tossed the stub of the cigarillo aside. "If I know outlaws, they'll be looking to spend a bit of it on whiskey, cards, and women."

Link looked confused. "How can we tell the stolen money from any other? Money's money."

Slocum stared toward the southwest, reading the lay of the land, mapping his next move in his mind. "The gold and silver the Tuckers kept in the big bank safe was new. Most of it was minted at Denver. Some was struck by Kansas. It's not unusual for states, territories, or even individual towns to mine and mint their own coin. If we find some new money with those mint marks, we'll know we're on the right trail."

Slocum glanced at the floodwaters below. The level was dropping fast. "Better mount up, Link. We don't want to lose too much time on the trail. I want to get across the Cimarron before dark."

Leather creaked as Link tightened the cinch on the black. "Won't the river be flooded, too, like this canyon?"

"Probably bank to bank and boiling like a witch's pot."

"How do we cross it?"

Slocum toed the stirrup and swung aboard his sorrel. "Very carefully," he said.

Ulysses Grant Abraham Lincoln stood naked on the south bank of the Cimarron and stared at the rolling red water beneath. He shivered despite the warmth of the sun on his drying skin.

His clothing and weapons lay wrapped in canvas bundles at his feet. His mind wouldn't let go of the terror that had clamped down on his gut during the crossing. It had started when he first looked down from the north bank at the raging waters, burrowed deeper when he followed Slocum's lead and stripped and secured the canvas packs. It chewed into his belly, almost a physical pain, as he clung to the saddle stirrup on the downstream side of the black as the horse swam the swift, boiling water.

"You all right, Link?"

Link glanced at Slocum. The tall man with the black hair and green eyes already had examined his weapons, found them dry and serviceable, and was climbing back into his clothes.

"I'm all right, Slocum," Link said. "I'm just—" he felt the rush of color to his face "—still scared, I guess."

"First river crossing?"

"You'll laugh."

Slocum buckled his gun belt into place. "I won't laugh, Link."

"I can't swim."

Slocum stared at Link for a moment. "Why didn't you tell me?"

"I was afraid you'd leave me behind. Or that we'd lose a day while you waited for the river to go down."

Slocum nodded. "You'll do, Link. A man who can face something like that without whining stands tall enough in my book. And don't apologize for being scared. Anyone with any common sense gets scared at times. Better tend your pack and get dressed."

Link reached for the canvas bundle at his feet. "Slocum, do you ever get scared?"

Slocum sat and pulled on a boot. "Sure I do," he said. "The trick is to face it down. Keep calm, stare fear in the face, and sooner or later it blinks." He tugged on the other boot and stood. "That, my young friend, is what separates the boys from the men in this world." Slocum stood and stared for a moment upriver. "Link," he said over his shoulder, "are you still carrying an empty chamber under the hammer of that Colt?"

Link glanced up, startled at the calm, cold tone of Slocum's voice. "Yes."

"Better slip that sixth round in. Could be trouble ahead."

Link hurried to finish dressing, then fed a cartridge into the empty chamber of his pistol. "What is it, Slocum?"

"Buzzards. About a half mile up the river. Circling a stand of cottonwoods."

"What do you reckon it is?" Link stamped into his boots, clapped his waterlogged hat on his head, and reached for the reins.

"We'll know soon enough," Slocum said. "Let's go."

Slocum knelt beside what was left of two men, the taste of bile heavy against the back of his throat. The coyotes and buzzards had stripped most of the flesh from the bodies. One man's face had been partly eaten away. The body cavities had been ripped open and the intestines devoured. The westering sun gleamed against the stark white of rib bones. Slocum stood and stared at the remains for a moment. He had seen all he needed to see. But he stalled, waiting for Link's retching to subside. Finally, he turned away.

Link leaned against the bole of a gnarled cottonwood, his face dead white, an arm pressed against his stomach. "Sorry, Slocum," Link gasped. "I never—saw anything like that—before."

"Quit apologizing, Link," Slocum said, his tone soft. "I've seen it before, and it still bothers me. God help us all if we ever get used to the sight." He took a deep breath and snorted the smell of death from his nostrils. "Both these men were shot in the head. Most likely Preacher Whiteside's work. Could have been anybody—there's a lot of bad hombres along the Strip—but I'd lay odds it was the man we're after who did this."

"Can you tell how long ago?"

"Day and a half, maybe two days," Slocum said. "The storm washed out most of the sign." He strode to his horse and mounted.

"Are we going to bury these men, Slocum?" Link asked.

Slocum shook his head. "Wouldn't help them any now. Mount up. We're heading upriver. Maybe we can cut some fresh sign along the way."

They had covered less than a mile before Slocum checked his mount and raised a hand. "Two horsemen up ahead, Link," he said. He tossed the lead rope of his pack horse to the young man. "Stay alert."

Link nodded, slipped the end of the lead rope beneath the cinch ring of his saddle, and tied it firmly.

The two men approached, horses at a slow trot, and pulled up a few feet from Slocum. He studied the pair. One was a hunched, toothless Mexican on a mouse-colored mustang. The other was a younger, bearded man on a big blood bay. The Mexican held an ancient .44 Henry rimfire rifle casually in the crook of an arm; the big man carried a sawed-off shotgun. Slocum noted that the hammers of the smoothbore already were eared back.

Slocum slouched in the saddle. "Afternoon," he said.

The Mexican nodded. "Good afternoon, my friends," he said in Spanish. "What brings you to the ranch of Juan Ortega?"

"Passing through. Headed for New Mexico." He kept his gaze locked on the face of the Mexican. The hunched man's dark eyes flicked over Slocum's sorrel, Link's black, and the two pack mounts. "You have some fine horses here, my friend."

"Thank you." Slocum forced a grin. "They'll do."

"What is your price for such animals?"

"They're not for sale," Slocum said.

The Mexican shrugged. "Ah, well, one must ask." Slocum saw the quick gleam in the man's eyes. He had seen that look. It usually showed just before guns started going off. The bearded man with the shotgun eased his horse off to one side, a good twenty feet from the old man. Slocum pulled himself erect in the saddle and chanced a glance at Link alongside.

"Think I'll step down and take a leak," Link said. His tone sounded casual enough. *The kid doesn't know what we're in for,* Slocum thought, *this is no time to take a piss.*

Link dismounted, turned away from the group, and started fumbling with his trouser buttons. Slocum focused his attention on the two horsemen. If it came to shooting, he had to pick his first target. That would be the man with the shotgun. The old Mexican might be quick enough to bring the rifle into play. Taking one man down was tough enough; taking both pushed the odds, but a man played the cards the way they fell. Slocum felt the familiar calm settle over his muscles.

"If the horses are not for sale," the hunched Mexican said, "perhaps you might wish to make us a gift of them?"

Slocum's eyes narrowed. "I think not," he said.

"A pity. There is so little generosity in the world these days. Good traveling, then, my friends." He started to rein his horse about; the motion swung the muzzle of the Henry toward Slocum's chest. At the corner of his vision Slocum saw the bearded man slap the shotgun to his shoulder.

Slocum's right hand snapped across his body and whipped the Colt from the holster; he thumbed the hammer back as he drew, let it slip as the muzzle swung into line. The Peacemaker slammed against Slocum's palm. The man with the shotgun twisted in the saddle as Slocum's slug took him with a heavy thump. Both barrels of the shotgun discharged, the thunderous roar almost atop the blast of Slocum's pistol. Buckshot whistled past Slocum's hat. Slocum's sorrel leapt sideways, snorting, startled at the sudden gunfire. The horse's movement turned Slocum's gun hand away from the Mexican. Slocum saw the distinct black hole in the bore of the Henry as the rifle fell into line. He braced himself for the bullet shock, knowing he would never get off an aimed shot before the Henry cracked.

The flat bark of a heavy pistol sounded at Slocum's right. The Mexican's body jerked; for a split second Slocum saw the look of disbelief in the man's eyes. The muzzle of the Henry dropped. Slocum brought his Colt into line and squeezed the trigger. The slug slammed the Mexican over the mustang's rump.

Slocum reined about toward the shotgunner. The man had dropped the weapon, slumped over the saddle horn as a red stain spread over his chest; he rammed spurs into his horse's ribs. The blood bay whirled and ran. Slocum snapped a shot and knew he had missed. Then the sharp crack of a big-bore rifle jarred Slocum's ears; the fleeing man tumbled from the saddle and fell. Dust spurted as his heavy torso hit the sandy soil.

Slocum glanced at Link. The young man levered a fresh round into the Winchester in his hands and stared toward the downed rider better than a hundred yards away. Link's face was pale, but his jaw was set, the rifle steady in firm hands. "Watch out, Link," Slocum said as he swung down from the nervous sorrel. "There might be some life left in them yet."

Slocum approached the downed Mexican with care. The hunched man's legs twitched and a groan came from his lips. *This is one tough old bird,* Slocum thought. He stuck the muzzle of his Colt into the old man's ear, plucked the scarred revolver from his belt, and tossed it aside. Link mounted and rode to the body of the shotgunner, stared down for a moment, and then reined his black back toward Slocum. "That one's dead, Slocum," Link said.

"This one isn't yet," Slocum said. "Thanks, Link. That was damned fine shooting. I owe you. This Mexican had me dead to rights with that Henry."

"I got lucky with the pistol, I guess," Link said. "First chance I had to go for the long gun, I took it."

Slocum rolled the Mexican's body over. The man's eyes were open, but glazed with pain and shock. Blood flowed from beneath his left arm. A slug had torn away part of a rib and ripped through the muscles before coming out his upper back. A second slug had taken him just above his belt. The belly wound would be the fatal one, Slocum knew at a glance. *Gut shot,* Slocum thought. *That's one damn tough way to die.* He had seen gut shot men in the war. Sometimes they lived for a week, suffering the agonies of the damned.

"Friend," Slocum said in Spanish, "before your time on this earth is over, I need some information. Have you seen a man called Whiteside? Tall, nose like a hawk, wears a frock coat and stovepipe hat."

"You—have killed me." The Mexican's voice was thin, reedy. He ran a tongue over his lips. "Water—for God's sake, water."

"Maybe later," Slocum said. "Now, have you seen the man I described?"

"Go—to hell—"

Slocum sighed. "Have it your way, friend." He rammed the muzzle of his pistol into the bloody patch above the man's belt. The Mexican cried out as a blast of agony swept through his body. Slocum waited until the eyes focused again. "Talk to me, or we will play Comanche and captive. I'll be the Comanche."

The Mexican tried to spit in Slocum's face. The bloody spittle dribbled down his chin.

"Link," Slocum called, "bring me that sack of salt from the pack."

Link was at his side a moment later, the small pouch in hand. "What are you going to do, Slocum?"

Slocum holstered his Colt and dribbled a few grains of salt into his palm. "Try to loosen this man's tongue a bit," he said. He trickled the salt into the belly wound. The Mexican screamed. Slocum waited until the peals of agony faded, then tapped a bit more salt into his palm. "Once again I ask, friend. Do you know this man Whiteside?"

"No—" The Mexican's pain-glazed eyes stared at Slocum's hand. Terror flickered beneath the agony. "In the name of God—"

Slocum dribbled more salt. The Mexican gasped and whimpered. Slocum knew the pain would be unbearable. And every man had his breaking point. He lifted the salt sack again.

"Wait—Mother of God—" The Mexican's words were barely audible through the grinding of his teeth. "He—was here. Two—two days ago."

"Where is he headed?"

Tears flowed freely down brown cheeks wrinkled by sun, wind, and age. "Chi—Chicota. Then—then to—Cimarron." The Mexican's voice grew weaker. "I know—nothing else."

Slocum nodded. "I'm glad you chose to help, friend," he said. "I hate wasting salt. It's damned expensive." He stood. "Link, see if you can catch this man's horse. I saw a canteen tied to his saddle." He turned back to the wounded man. "We will leave you water," he said. "You know how long it takes a gut shot man to die. Rest in peace."

The Mexican grasped weakly at Slocum's pants leg. "For God's sake—kill me—the pain—"

"Can't do that, friend," Slocum said, "but maybe I can help you a little bit." He strode to the fallen Henry rifle, worked the action to eject the cartridges, and tossed all but one into the brush nearby. He dropped the last cartridge into his pocket, then placed the weapon at the Mexican's side.

Link rode up, leading the mouse-colored mustang. Slocum untied the canteen and tossed it onto the dying man's chest. "Come on, Link," he said. "We have some riding to do."

Moments later Slocum stopped at a lightning-ravaged cottonwood fifty feet from the moaning Mexican. He dug the single Henry cartridge from his pocket and placed it in the splintered trunk of the tree. "If you can reach it, friend," he said, "here is your release from a long and painful death." He kneed his horse into motion, Link riding alongside.

"Like I said before, Link, you'll do," Slocum said. "I thought you were getting us both in trouble when you said you had to take a leak. I didn't know you had a play in mind."

Link glanced at Slocum. "We both know I don't shoot worth a damn from horseback, Slocum. It was the only way I could figure to help out." He fell silent for a few minutes, his brow wrinkled in thought, as the two men rode past the dead man in the trail. Link looked back at the body. "Slocum," Link finally said, "I just killed a man. Shot him in the back with a Winchester when he was trying to run away. I don't feel so good about that. Seems like it wasn't fair."

Slocum flashed a quick, reassuring grin at his young saddle mate. "And if you hadn't shot him, he might have ambushed us by now. You did just fine. And, Link, remember this: There is no such thing as a fair fight. When somebody's trying to kill you, your only choice is to take him down first. Any way you can." Slocum reached for a cigarillo. "That man picked his own road, Link. He picked the wrong one. Don't stew your guts about it."

They had covered almost a half mile before the crack of a rifle sounded in the distance. Slocum shook his head in admiration. "That was one tough man." He turned to study his young companion's face. Link was beginning to get his color back. A few moments later Link pulled his horse to a stop.

"Problem, son?"

"All of a sudden," Link said, "I really *have* got to take a piss."

Chicota was a time-worn cluster of adobe huts not far from the headwaters of the Cimarron. Slocum had seen many such communities in the past. Chicota was a town waiting to die. All that kept it alive now were the Mexican shepherds who ran their small flocks along the river breaks. Slocum knew that soon even that trade would wither. The cattlemen in northern New Mexico and the Texas Panhandle would move in to take over the grazing lands. The cattlemen hated sheep herders almost as much as they hated sheep.

He reined his sorrel to a stop before a run-down adobe. The building had no sign posted, but the smell of sawdust and liquor wafted from the door. Slocum needed a drink and information, and the best place to find both in a small town was the cantina. He dismounted and looped the sorrel's reins over a sagging hitch rail. Link followed suit.

Slocum stepped inside and waited a few seconds until his eyes adapted to the dimness inside the cantina. He scanned the sparse gathering of drinkers, saw no one who appeared to be the sort who would ride with Preacher Whiteside, and strode to the bar. Link followed, the sound of his spur rowels muted on the hard-packed dirt floor with its smattering of sawdust.

A plump Mexican woman stood behind the bar, wiping a glass with a soiled rag. She raised a questioning eyebrow. *"Dos cervezas, dos whiskeys,"* Slocum said. He fished a coin from his pocket and tossed it on the stained planks of the crude pine bar. The woman filled two mugs from a keg and dribbled whiskey into shot glasses. Slocum sipped at the beer. It was strong, malty, and lukewarm, but it cut the travel dust. He tossed back the whiskey and winced. It was trade whiskey, probably colored by tobacco juice, and it was the worst he had tasted in years.

He waved the woman closer. She leaned forward, resting huge breasts on the bar. "More whiskey?"

Slocum shook his head. "I'm looking for a man," he said in Spanish. "Short, heavyset. Scar on his face, one eye. He would have two bullet holes in him."

The woman's dense black eyebrows bunched in thought. Slocum noticed she had a distinct mustache, black hairs darkening a puffy upper lip. Stretch marks left white streaks against the dark skin of her upper breasts. *Glad I'm not looking for a woman on this stop,* Slocum thought. *I'm not that desperate yet.* "I do not know of such a man," she said.

Slocum pulled a gold double eagle from his pocket and held it before him. "Perhaps your memory could be prodded a bit? This man I seek would be in the company of others. One is a tall man who wears a frock coat and tall hat."

The woman stared at the coin for a moment, the expression in her eyes like that of a starving man ogling a thick steak. Twenty dollars American was probably more than she had seen in years, Slocum thought. The woman shifted her gaze to Slocum's face.

"Perhaps, now that I think of it, there were such men here," she said. "Day before yesterday, I think it was. The one-eyed man seemed ill. He stayed on his horse outside. The tall one came in."

Slocum toyed with the gold piece, tantalizing the woman. "Do you know where they are now?"

She shrugged. "The tall one asked if we had a doctor. He did not seem pleased when we told him we did not, that the nearest real healer was in Cimarron. He bought three bottles of whiskey. Paid in silver, then left."

"Was it new silver?"

The woman nodded. She turned away, rummaged in a ragged box, and handed a coin to Slocum. It was shiny, new, and it bore the stamp of the Denver mint. Slocum handed the coin back to the woman, then slid the double eagle onto the counter. "Thank you for your help," he said.

The woman flashed a stained, leering grin as the coin disappeared somewhere into the canyon of cleavage. "Perhaps I might help in other ways?"

Slocum shook his head. "Not this time, señorita," he said pleasantly, "unless my friend here is in need of some service."

"What's going on, Slocum?" Link asked. "I don't speak Spanish all that well yet."

Slocum grinned at the young man. "This woman has offered to take you to her bed, Link—for a price. It would probably be cheap enough, if you're interested."

Link's face turned scarlet in embarrassment. He dropped his eyes from the big woman to stare at his glass. "Tell her thanks for the offer, but I'm much too busy at the moment," he said. He tossed back his shot of whiskey, almost gagged on the raw liquor, and glanced anxiously toward the door.

Slocum translated Link's message, pleased that his young friend had shown the tact not to insult the woman. For all he knew, she might speak perfect English, and it wasn't polite to insult a woman, even a fat, ugly whore.

Slocum finished his beer, touched fingers to hat brim in salute to the woman, and led the way from the cantina. He paused for a moment in the late afternoon sun, staring south toward Cimarron.

"What now, Slocum? What did you find out?"

"They were here, all right. The descriptions fit, and that coin just about had to come from the Scott's Ford bank job." Slocum fished a cigarillo from his pocket and fired the smoke with a lucifer. "The woman said they headed for Cimarron when they left here."

"How far is that?"

Slocum shrugged. "Day's ride, more or less."

Link strode toward the hitch rail where his black stood hipshot and dozing. "Let's go, Slocum."

Slocum raised a hand. "Now's not the time to get antsy, Link. Our horses are tired, we don't have much daylight left, and we're running short on supplies. We'll overnight here. There should be at least a boardinghouse and a stable in this town."

Link whirled to face Slocum. His amber eyes flashed in disgust and anger. "Dammit, Slocum! Are we going to just fart around until it's too late to catch them?"

Slocum took a drag on the cigarillo and squinted through the smoke. "We'll catch up, Link. You ever watch a cougar stalk a deer?"

"What the hell's that got to do with anything?"

"Everything, Link. If the big cat hurries, it makes a mistake. The deer hears it or smells it and gets away. But if the cougar's patient, stalks the deer a step at a time, the deer winds up dead." He let smoke trickle from his nostrils. "We're the cougars. If we jump too quick, it won't be the deer we're after who wind up dead. If we make a mistake, son, they'll kill Victoria for sure. And maybe you and me to boot."

"But, Slocum—"

Slocum pinned a hard glare on his companion's face. "Link, you promised not to argue when we started this. You've made a good enough hand so far. But we play it my way, or you ride back to Kansas. Is that clear?"

The tension slowly drained from Link's face. He sighed and his shoulders drooped. "Clear enough, Slocum. I know damn well you could do without me. I can't do without you. I'll shut up and follow orders."

"Good. Now, let's find us a room, get the animals tended, buy some supplies, and get a night's sleep in a real bed. Maybe the cooties won't be too bad." Slocum reached out and put a reassuring hand on Link's shoulder.

"Don't worry, son," he said. "We'll get her back." He paused for a moment, trying to think of the right words. "Link, I've got to ask you a question. When we get her back, she might be—different. It's a possibility you have to face. Could you handle it if those men decided to pass her around a bit?"

Link stared into Slocum's eyes. "I could handle that," he said softly. "I love the girl, Slocum. I've already thought that out. It doesn't matter. I want her back." His tone turned tight and hard. "But I'll kill every one of the dirty bastards if they do anything to her."

Slocum let his hand fall away. "That's what I wanted to hear, Link. Now, let's get a move on. We'll be on our way to Cimarron at first light."

7

Dealing in stolen livestock wasn't the only industry in Cimarron, New Mexico, Slocum reminded himself as he reined his horse onto the dusty main street, but rustling was way ahead of other business conducted in the cluster of adobe and stone buildings of the thriving town.

The outpost, nestled in the San Juan Mountain Range, drew outlaws, gamblers, and whores from a half dozen states or territories and the Cimarron Strip like a honey pot drew flies. Few men who carried a badge ventured into the northern reaches of New Mexico. The climate here was not conducive to long lives among lawmen.

But, Slocum thought, the whiskey had to be better here. It couldn't get any worse than that sheep-dip served up at Chicota. He reined his sorrel toward the public livery stable at the northeast edge of town. Link followed, leading the pack animals, his amber eyes sweeping the adobe-lined streets. *The kid's learning,* Slocum thought. *He's started to pay attention to where he is and where somebody else might be.*

And somewhere in this town, one or more of the men they sought should be waiting. The idea sharpened Slocum's senses and brought the relaxed tension back to his muscles. He pulled his mount to a stop in front of the stable.

"Anybody here?" Slocum called.

Moments later a stooped, aging Mexican limped into view. *"Sí, señor?* You wish to board some horses?"

"Maybe," Slocum answered casually. "First, I'd like some information, if it is known to you." He reached into a pocket for a five-dollar gold piece and held it aloft. "This will be in your pocket if you have the knowledge I seek."

The hostler nodded, his gaze on the coin. "Perhaps I can be of service. If you wish to find the best whores, the honest card games, the uncut whiskey, I will be your devoted guide."

"My friend and I are looking for a man. He would have others with him. This man is a stocky fellow. He has but one eye, a scar on his face, and a couple of reasonably fresh bullet holes in him. He travels with a group led by a tall man who wears a frock coat and stovepipe hat."

The Mexican glanced about, nervous fingers stroking a scraggly goatee. "This man you seek is here. He rode in day before yesterday, with the tall one in the strange hat. There were six men and a girl—"

"The girl," Link interrupted, "was she all right?"

"Yes, I think, but she look worried, maybe scared," the Mexican said. "An hour later, four men and the girl ride out. They left behind the man who had been shot, and another who I think was the wounded one's friend."

"Where might we find these two men who stayed behind?"

The Mexican cleared his throat. "They will kill me if they know I tell you. I do not know that one gold coin is worth such a gamble."

"They'll never know, friend." Slocum reached for another gold piece. "Perhaps two coins would weigh more than the risk."

The hostler grinned, showing gapped and stained teeth, and dropped the coins in a frayed pocket. "The men you seek are in the St. Joseph Hotel. They sent for the doctor to tend the wounded one." The Mexican sighed and shook his head. "I think the one-eyed man will die soon."

Slocum's smile was cold. "It is my most fervent wish, friend," he said. "I am the man who shot him." He waited until the startled expression faded from the hostler's heavily lined face. "Did they leave their horses here?"

The Mexican nodded.

"Saddle one of them and bring it to me."

"Only one?"

"Yes. You may keep the other horse, along with the saddle and equipment. Consider it a bonus. For your silence," Slocum added pointedly.

The hostler swallowed, his eyes wide, and shuffled away. He reappeared a few minutes later leading a rangy brown, a worn saddle strapped into place. Slocum mounted, took the reins from the hostler, and nodded to Link. "Let's go. It's hunting time."

Slocum and Link rode at a slow trot down Cimarron's main street and reined in before a two-story adobe. A weathered sign above the door read "St. Joseph Hotel." Slocum swung down and hitched the horses. The two men strode into the hotel, spur rowels jingling on rough pine flooring. Slocum paused for a moment to let his eyes adjust to the near-gloom inside the building, then sauntered to the innkeeper's desk. A drowsy-looking man looked up from the hand of solitaire spread atop the desk.

"Need a room, gents?"

"No," Slocum said. "We're looking for a couple of men who are staying here. One's called Jubal. Don't know the other one's name. What room are they in?"

The clerk's eyes narrowed. "Now, I ain't too sure I ought to tell you that—" The protest ended in a choked squawk as Slocum reached out, grabbed a handful of shirt, and yanked the man halfway across the desk.

"Mister, I'm a little short of time and plumb out of patience," Slocum said, his tone icy. "Now, where are they?"

"Room—six. Top of stairs—on left." The clerk gasped for air as Slocum released his hold.

"Stay out of this and keep quiet," Slocum warned, "or they'll be finding pieces of you all over this hotel." He glanced at the solitaire hand spread on the desk. "Black queen on the red king," he said. "Get back to your game. And keep your hands on the cards."

Slocum spun on a heel and strode toward the stairs, Link a step behind. At the doorway to room six, Slocum and Link pulled their pistols. Link flattened himself against the wall. The young man's jaw was firm and his eyes alert.

Slocum raised a boot and kicked. The door latch shattered under the impact; Slocum was in the room before the startled man seated beside the bed could reach for the pistol on the table nearby. The bore of Slocum's Colt pointed between the swarthy man's eyes.

"What the hell—"

"Make a move for that gun, mister, and you're dead as last year's hog," Slocum said. He waited until the man raised his hands, then sidled up to the bedside stand, lifted the pistol from the table, and thrust it in his waistband.

"What are you doing here?"

"Shut up," Slocum snapped. "Link, keep this man covered. If he so much as farts, blow his brains out."

Slocum leaned over the bed where the man called Jubal lay, his body swathed in bandages. His breathing was shallow and erratic. Bloody froth speckled the corner of slack lips. Jubal was unconscious. Slocum casually poked the muzzle of his Colt into the bandage over Jubal's shoulder. The one-eyed man moaned and stirred, but did not open his eyes.

"Looks like your partner here has about bought the farm," Slocum said. "But then, he's pretty tough. He might live. I'd sure hate to hear about that." Slocum clamped a hand over the wounded man's mouth and nose and squeezed. Jubal's eyes fluttered open; he struggled weakly against the death grip, fingers scratching at Slocum's hand, trying to draw air. After a few moments, the struggles stopped. Slocum slid his hand inside the wounded man's shirt. There was no heartbeat.

Slocum stood, satisfied. He turned to the swarthy man, stepped forward, and rapped the barrel of his handgun against the man's temple. The man's knees buckled. He dropped, unconscious. Slocum stepped over the body, plucked a pair of saddlebags from the corner, and slung them over his shoulder. "Grab his other arm," Slocum said to Link as he slid a hand beneath the downed man's armpit. "Let's get out of here, quick and quiet. We'll take care of him later."

The two dragged the unconscious man down the stairs, past the wide-eyed hotel clerk, and heaved him onto the back of the spare horse. Slocum mounted and held the swarthy man in the saddle as Link gathered the lead ropes of the pack animals. Ten minutes later they were headed south from Cimarron, moving at a quick trot.

The sun was two hours above the western horizon before Slocum called a halt in a secluded canyon eight miles south of Cimarron.

The swarthy man had regained consciousness. He sat on the spare horse, hands bound. He supported his weight on the saddle horn and glared at Slocum. One eye was swollen almost shut and blood trickled from the gash left by the whack of Slocum's gun barrel. "Who the hell are you? What you want?" The voice was still a bit croaky.

"Name's Slocum. I'm a collector. Collecting members of Preacher Whiteside's bunch at the moment." Slocum's voice was calm and matter-of-fact. "You have a name?"

"Clell Bates. I don't know nobody name of Whiteside."

"Like hell you don't," Link said, his tone sharp. "Half a dozen people saw you ride out of Scott's Ford with Whiteside."

"You don't know what you're talkin' about, you little whelp," Bates muttered.

"Let me refresh your memory a bit," Slocum said pleasantly. "When Whiteside hit that bank up in Kansas they killed a friend of mine along with a bank teller. They took a young girl hostage. I want the rest of the gang, Bates. And the girl. You're going to tell me where to find them."

"The hell I am." Bates pursed his lips and spat. The spittle plopped against Slocum's boot. Slocum glanced at the glob, then casually wiped his boot toe against a sage clump.

"Have it your way," Slocum said with a shrug. He strode to his sorrel and slipped the tie-down thong from his rope. He glanced around the small clearing and spotted a tall cottonwood with a thick limb about ten feet off the ground. He reached for the reins of Bates's horse.

"What the—what the hell you doing?" The unswollen eye widened in sudden fear, the defiance gone, as Slocum led Bates's horse beneath the limb.

"Just a little friendly lynching, Clell," Slocum said. "Nothing to get yourself all worked up about." He tossed the noose end over the limb, grabbed the loop, and tapped it against a palm. "Now, Clell. Tell me where Whiteside is and where he's headed."

Bates glanced up at the limb, then at the rope in Slocum's hand. His face went pale. "My God, man—you can't—"

Slocum tossed the loop around Bates's neck and pulled it snug with a flip of the wrist. "Like hell I can't, Clell." His tone was hard and flinty. "I can, and I will, and I'll enjoy it. Now, where's Whiteside?"

"For God's sake, Slocum! No rope! I'll tell you! Just let me go!" The words tumbled from lips gone slack with terror.

"So talk to me, Clell. Then I'll think it over." As he spoke, Slocum tied the loose end of the rope snug around the tree trunk with a slipknot.

"South! Preacher's headed south!"

Slocum tugged at the rope. He had left about a foot and a half of slack between the noose around Bates's neck and the tree limb overhead. "Not good enough, Clell. Where to, exactly?"

"Helltown—" Spittle sprayed from Bates's lips. "He took—Helltown Trail."

"How many men does he have?"

"Four—four now—said he'd pick up more men—Pope's Crossing on the Pecos." A stain spread over Bates's crotch. *This is one mighty scared man,* Slocum thought. *He's gone and pissed in his pants already.*

"The girl. Is she all right? Has anybody decided to help themselves to a piece of her yet?" Slocum glanced at Link and saw the young man wince in pain at the question.

"No! Preacher—he said don't nobody touch her—called her virgin of Babbylion—somethin' like that."

"Where's your share of the bank job money, Bates?"

"Preacher's still got it. He give me a hundred to get Jubal doctored. What's left of the hundred's in them saddlebags. Take it." Bates's voice went up a notch. "You got to let me go now, Slocum! We had a deal—"

"We didn't have a deal, Clell," Slocum said. "I told you I'd think about it. I've thought about it." He stepped behind

Bates's horse, swept his hat from his head, and slapped it against the animal's rump. The horse bolted. Clell Bates's cry choked off as the noose snapped taut around his neck. The outlaw's feet flailed the air, searching for a toehold, bound hands clawing at the noose embedded in his neck. In a few minutes, the twitching stopped. Slocum smelled the foul odor as the man's sphincter let go.

Slocum studied Link's face as Bates's body turned slowly at the end of the rope. Bates's face was almost black, the tongue swollen and purple, protruding from lips still twisted in the grimace of death. Link was pale, his mouth drawn into a fine line, as he stared at the outlaw's body.

"God, Slocum." Link's voice was soft. "I've never seen a man hanged before."

"Not a pretty sight," Slocum said. "Never got used to it, myself. Hope I never do. But if it's any consolation, the bastard deserved it." He reached in his pocket, pulled out a cigarillo, and fired the smoke. "You going to throw up on me, son?"

Link swallowed hard. "No. Like you say, I suppose he deserved it." The young man shuddered. "Jesus, what a rotten way to die."

Slocum shrugged. "There are no good ways to die, Link." He dragged smoke deep into his lungs, exhaled through his nostrils, and strode to his horse. He had tossed Bates's saddlebags over the sorrel's withers. He opened one of the bags, lifted out a couple of coins, and grunted in satisfaction. The silver was new and bore the stamp of the Kansas mint.

"Slocum?"

Slocum clamped the cigarillo in his teeth and squinted through the smoke at Link. "Yes?"

"Are we going to just leave him here—like that?"

"Nope. That's my rope around his neck. Good Manila hemp's expensive and hard to find." He strode to the tree and yanked at the loose end of the rope. The slipknot came free. Clell Bates's body hit the ground with a solid thump. Slocum had to yank twice at the loop embedded in Bates's neck before the hemp pulled free. He re-coiled the rope and headed for his sorrel.

"Link, I hope your butt's toughened up over the last few days," Slocum said as he mounted. "It's time to start closing ground on Whiteside, and it's a long ride from here to Helltown."

Link glanced back over his shoulder once as they rode from the clearing. He was silent for almost an hour. "Slocum," he finally said, "what's this Helltown?"

Slocum's eyes narrowed as he studied the trail ahead. "Outlaw hangout just across the Rio Grande from Presidio. One of the meanest spots on the face of the earth. If we don't catch up with Whiteside's bunch before they get there, we'll have one hell of a time digging them out. There's always a couple of dozen gunhands hanging around Helltown."

Slocum glanced at the lowering sun. "We'll strike Helltown Trail about sundown. The trail mostly follows the Pecos River down through New Mexico into Texas, then cuts through the Davis Mountains to the Chihuahua Road and on into Presidio. It's a long ride through rough country. We'll rest the horses a while, wait for moonrise, and ride out most of the night. From here on in, Link, keep your eyes open and your hand close to a gun."

"Slocum? What's going to happen to Victoria? If we don't catch up with them before Helltown, I mean?"

Slocum sighed. "God only knows, Link. I guess a lot of that's up to Victoria."

Victoria Tucker huddled closer to the campfire and tried to ignore the pressure of Jeb Dawson's glare against her shoulder blades.

The night air of the lower Pecos River desert country had turned cool, but that wasn't what brought the chill to her bones. It was the constant tension of not knowing what the next hour might bring. Ten days on the trail with little sleep had taxed her physical strength. And she needed a bath. She had never felt so grubby in her life, she thought as she stared at her chipped and ragged fingernails.

The worry and fear that gnawed at her belly had grown worse over the last three days. At least a dozen times she thought she had seen a chance to escape, only to have the opportunity crushed. Preacher watched her like a hawk, even when she had to answer nature's calls. She had grown accustomed to his disinterested presence, but not to the embarrassment of having a man watch her in what should have been private moments.

And now, Preacher's gang was about to pick up reinforcements. The men hadn't been secretive about their plans. Pope's Crossing was only two days' ride ahead, and there three more men would join the group. Victoria didn't recall the names, but she remembered the way Preacher had described their talents: fast with a gun and meaner than a badger with a headache, he had said. Victoria knew that she had to make her bid to escape before the gang reached Pope's Crossing. She might be able to get away from four men, but never from seven—

She started at the sound of a step behind her and glanced over her shoulder. The surge of fear passed in a heartbeat. Dade Fowler stood there, a blanket in his hand.

"Sorry if I scared you, Victoria," Fowler said, "but I thought you might be needing this." He held out the blanket. It was worn and soiled, but Victoria took it gratefully and wrapped it about her shoulders.

"Sit with me a moment, Dade," she said. "I—I feel so much safer when you're nearby. That awful Dawson frightens me so. The way he looks at me makes me feel dirty inside."

Fowler squatted beside her and stared into the flames. "Try not to worry about him too much," Fowler said. "He knows he'd have to go through Preacher to get to you. And I think he's beginning to suspect he'd have to go through me, too." He lifted his gaze to Victoria's eyes. "I don't know if I can stop him if that happens, but I promise you I'll do my best."

Victoria let a smile crease her chapped lips. "Thank you, Dade." She touched a hand to his forearm. "You'll never know how much that means to me. At the same time, I don't want to see you hurt."

Fowler fell silent for a moment. His gaze seemed tender, protective, as he stared at Victoria. Then he frowned. "Victoria, I don't like the way things are shaping up," he said, his voice barely above a whisper. "Preacher's started acting funny. He's nervous. He's been watching our back trail, like he thinks there's someone following us. And the look in his eyes—well, I don't know how to describe it, but I've heard he gets awfully twitchy when he starts to come out of these religious spells."

Victoria felt a chill shudder up her spine. "Dade, if he does change, what will happen?"

"I don't know. I've heard he turns even crazier. As if he weren't loco enough already." Fowler turned his gaze back to the fire, his brow wrinkled in thought. "We've got to get out of here, Victoria," he said. "I think I've come up with a way—" His words stopped abruptly at the sound of heavy footsteps on the sand behind them.

"Hey, pretty boy." Jeb Dawson stood three strides away, his thumbs hooked into his belt, a heavy scowl turning the scars on his face a livid pink.

Dade Fowler stood and turned to face Dawson, his hands balled into fists at his side. "Are you talking to me, Dawson?"

"Damn right I am. What the hell you doin'? Shinin' up to the filly? By God, I got my brand on her, Fowler. When the time comes to stick this gal, I'm the one who's gonna do the stickin'." The swarthy face twisted into an outright leer. "Damn fine tits and ass on that young mare. I ain't gonna see 'em wasted on no pretty boy like you."

Dade Fowler stared at Dawson for a few heartbeats, then shrugged. He stared to turn away, then suddenly spun on a heel and slammed his right fist into the bridge of Dawson's nose. Dawson staggered back a step, more surprised than hurt at the blow. Fowler followed and ripped a solid left into Dawson's gut. Dawson barked an enraged curse and swung a hamlike fist. The heavy blow caught Fowler on the side of the head. Fowler stumbled backward and almost went down.

Victoria scrambled free of the fracas and came to her feet. Her heart skidded as Dawson's hand darted to his belt; the firelight glinted on steel.

"Watch out, Dade! He's got a knife!" Victoria called.

Fowler crouched, poised on the balls of his feet, obviously stunned from the impact of Dawson's fist. Dawson took a step forward, waving the knife at belt height, a trickle of blood seeping from his nose. "You little bastard, I'm gonna gut you like I was butcherin' a steer, now."

"Hold it!" The call startled Victoria; she hadn't seen the half-breed with the smoke-colored eyes approach. Dirk Campbell stepped between the two men. "That's enough, Jeb. You too, Dade. Both of you calm down. You know Preacher's rules. No fighting among ourselves."

"Damn you, you half-breed son of a bitch, get out of my way," Dawson growled. "I'm going to geld this skinny little bastard."

"No, you won't, Jeb," Campbell said, his tone soft but deadly. "If you want a knife fight, try me." His hand drifted to the haft of the big bowie at his belt.

Dawson hesitated. The rage drained from his face. Wariness flickered in his eyes. "I got no quarrel with you, Dirk," he said. "And I ain't gonna cross blades with you. I seen what you can do with that damn ax you call a knife. But you mark my words, this ain't over between him and me."

Dirk Campbell shrugged. "Maybe not. But it won't be finished in this camp. We need every gun we have until we cross the Rio Grande. Jeb, go relieve Preacher on watch." The half-breed turned his back on Dawson. "Dade, you go check on the horses. Both of you settle down."

"Who died and made you boss?" Dawson growled. But despite the parting sarcasm, the stocky man turned and strode away.

Dade Fowler hesitated, glancing first at Victoria and then at Campbell. Then, without speaking, he rubbed a hand across his bruised temple and disappeared into the darkness.

The half-breed turned to Victoria. "Are you all right, miss?"

Victoria swallowed against the tightness in her throat and nodded. "I'm all right. Thank you for stopping it before someone was hurt or killed."

Firelight sparkled in the expressionless gray eyes. "Miss Tucker, take a word of advice. Don't play games with these men." He turned and strode from the circle of light and seemed to simply disappear into the darkness.

Victoria stood for a moment, shivering as the last of the fear drained from her body, and stared at the spot where the night had swallowed the half-breed. *He knows,* she thought. *He knows what I've been trying to do. Did he overhear Dade's whisper that there might be a way?* And the even bigger question: Had Dirk Campbell confided his suspicions to Preacher Whiteside?

Whether the cadaverous Preacher knew or not, Victoria decided, she had no choice. She had to escape, or die trying.

Slocum reined his tired sorrel onto the main street of Eddy, New Mexico, the last oasis in the mostly dry flatness of the southern Staked Plains, and tried to blink the weariness from eyes hammered by days of sun, wind, and sand.

Slocum was tired, hot, dirty, thirsty, and worried.

They had gained less than a day on Whiteside's band despite pushing their horses to the limit. Eighteen hours a day in the saddle, stopping only to switch horses, and still they lagged far behind their prey. Now they stood to lose a few more hours replenishing supplies, resting the horses, and telegraphing Scott's Ford for more expense money. If Clell Bates hadn't been lying, Whiteside would beat them to Pope's Crossing. Instead of four guns they would be facing seven, maybe more, dangerous men in the final moments of the chase. It wasn't something that sat easy on Slocum's mind.

At his side Link rode erect and alert in the saddle, his gaze flicking about the buildings and alleys that slid past the two hunters. The kid had toughened to the saddle and his hands were now callused from practice with the big Colt on his hip. He seemed to have fallen into Slocum's own habit of riding without talking. *I guess I don't have to worry about Link's being able to back me up any longer,* Slocum thought. *You learn a lot about a man in over a week on the trail.* Slocum liked what he had learned about the greenhorn from back East. By now he could almost forgive young Ulysses Grant Abraham Lincoln for having four Yankee names.

Slocum pulled his horse to a stop before the only two-story building in town. The building was made of real lumber, not the adobe prevalent in Eddy, and it was freshly whitewashed. A new sign across the front proclaimed the establishment to be the Roundup Saloon. A half dozen horses stood hitched at the rail. He dismounted and raised an eyebrow at Link. "You've earned a drink, son," he said. "I'm going to see if I can dig out some information here."

Link shook his head. "I'll take the horses on to the stable and get them tended, then find a store."

Slocum nodded, jiggled the Colt in its holster to make sure it would ride free in case it was needed, and tossed the reins to Link. "Keep track of the expenses," Slocum said. "I've got a feeling Will Tucker might not take our word about just how much this hunt's costing."

Slocum stood for a moment and watched as the young man led the sorrel and two pack animals away, then stepped into the saloon.

The Roundup was cleaner than most others Slocum had visited. There was only a faint odor of beer, whiskey, sweat, and tobacco smoke in the cool air. Slocum stood by the door until his vision had adjusted to the dim interior, then strode to the bar.

He motioned to the barkeep, ordered a shot of Old Overholt and a beer. He downed the shot, drank a third of the cool beer without coming up for air, then let his gaze drift around the saloon. The place was about half full. Most of the drinkers were obviously cowpunchers in town for a rare day off the range. He saw no familiar faces.

Slocum waved to the bartender. "Do you know a man called Preacher Whiteside?"

The barkeep, a thick-chested, middle-aged man with a scar running through one eyebrow, leaned against the bar and stared at Slocum with interest. "You a friend of his, mister?"

Slocum's eyes narrowed. "Not exactly. I'm the man who plans to kill him."

The barkeep seemed to relax. "Good luck to you, then. I saw Whiteside once, about three years back, up in the Dakotas. He's hard to forget. Spooky-looking fellow. Heard he rides with a bunch of mighty tough men."

"Has he been in town over the last few days?"

The bartender scratched at the scarred eyebrow. "Don't think so. Most everybody who comes to town drifts by here sooner or later." He reached for a bottle and refilled Slocum's glass. "Sorry I can't tell you anything more." The barkeep strode away to tend the needs of other customers.

Slocum sipped at the drink, lost in his thoughts. Whatever else he was, Preacher Whiteside had a way with men. Any other gang would have split up long ago, in a hurry to spend the money burning their pockets. But only a scattering of the distinctive coins had turned up between here and Kansas. And even though he and Link had stopped at every trading post and town from the Cimarron all the way down the Pecos, there had been no indication that Whiteside or any of his men had stopped for supplies. They had to be running low on staples by now. A group of men on the dodge couldn't come this far without using up a fair amount of bacon, salt, sugar, beans, and whiskey. Especially whiskey. *Preacher's got to be hurting some,* Slocum concluded. *Maybe he'll make a mistake soon. If he does, we'll be ready.*

Slocum finished his drink, tossed a coin on the counter, and strode from the saloon into the late afternoon sun that beat down on the dusty street. The gusty wind from the southwest swirled trash and dust around buildings and into the doorways and alleys.

He found Link at the general store a block from the saloon, tallying expenses in a small record book as he checked over a pile of supplies on the counter. Slocum plucked a dozen cigarillos and a box of matches from the tobacco case. "Might as well add these to the tab, Link," he said, "and throw in a couple of quarts of good whiskey. We might as well travel in comfort."

Link nodded, made a couple of notes in the record book, then turned to the storekeeper. "We'll be wanting to leave our purchases in the store overnight. We'll pick them up at dawn tomorrow."

"But, sir," the clerk said, "we don't open until after eight o'clock."

Link glared hard at the clerk. "You will tomorrow." It wasn't a request, Slocum noted; it was a simple statement. The clerk swallowed and nodded. *The kid's getting a handle on how things get done.*

The two hunters strode from the general store and ambled toward the one-story hotel a few doors down. A tall, rangy man with pale eyes stepped from a small office and nodded a greeting. "Hello, Slocum."

Slocum returned the nod. He did not offer a hand.

"Going to be in town long?" The tall man's eyes held a glint of suspicion tinged with grudging respect.

"Just overnight," Slocum said. He gestured toward the young man at his side. "Link, meet Pat Garrett, sheriff of Lincoln County."

Slocum glanced at Link. The young man's eyes were wide in surprise and awe. Link offered a hand. "I've heard a lot about you, Sheriff Garrett," he said. Garrett returned the handshake, but he didn't take his eyes from Slocum.

"What brings you two to Eddy?" Garrett asked.

"Hunting, you might say," Slocum said.

"Anybody I know?"

"Preacher Whiteside and his bunch."

Garrett's eyebrows went up, a sudden flash of interest displacing the suspicion in his eyes. "Pretty tough game you're tracking there, Slocum. This have anything to do with a telegram I got over in Lincoln a while back?"

Slocum nodded, reached in his pocket for two cigarillos, and offered one to the lawman. Garrett took the tobacco with a nod of thanks, nipped the end off the cigarillo, and dug a match from a shirt pocket. "Whiteside's got something of ours," Slocum said. "We want it back."

Garrett fired the match, cupped it in a hand to shield it from the wind, and offered the light to Slocum. Slocum dipped his head, puffed the cigarillo into life, and dragged at the rich tobacco. Garrett lit his own, then shook the lucifer out, squeezed the head, and broke the stick before tossing it aside.

"Any word about Whiteside being around here, Pat?"

Garrett shook his head. "Haven't seen him. But three men rode in here this morning. Tough hombres. Jesús Quintana, Stony Lollar, and Buck Teague. I hear those three are compadres of Whiteside."

Slocum winced inwardly. He knew Quintana personally, firsthand and over gunsights, and he had heard of the other two. All three men were poison with handguns, reckless and violent. "They still around?"

"Nope," Garrett said. "I asked them to ride on out. Thought for a minute they might decide to argue about it." A thin smile lifted the sheriff's narrow lips. "It's possible the sawed-off ten-bore I was holding at the time helped change their minds. Should have put them in irons, I guess, but I didn't have warrants on them."

"Looks like Preacher's padding his hand with some aces," Slocum said.

"Looks like it." Garrett took a long drag at the cigarillo and raised an eyebrow at Slocum. "You want some help? I know a few men around here who wouldn't mind seeing Whiteside facedown over a saddle."

Slocum rolled the cigarillo in his fingers. "I reckon not, Pat. Link and I can handle it."

"Well, good luck to you," Garrett said. "I'd like to be on this hunt myself, but I've got a prisoner to haul back to Lincoln tomorrow." The six-foot-five lawman touched fingers to his hat brim in salute. "Watch your ass out there, Slocum. That's a bad bunch." Garrett turned and strode away down the wind-whipped street.

"Damn," Link said softly, "I never thought I'd meet a man like him. The newspapers and books back East are full of stories about Pat Garrett." The awe was plain in Link's voice. "Slocum, is he as good with a gun as I've heard?"

"Good enough, Link. He's a dead shot, especially with a long gun. Learned that as a buffalo hunter before he pinned on a badge."

"Is he as good as you are?"

Slocum stared toward the lanky figure in the near distance. "I don't think either one of us is real anxious to find out, Link," he said. "Come on. Let's get some chuck and a good night's sleep in a real bed." He cocked his head toward his companion. "You want a woman tonight? They've got all kinds in Eddy."

Link shook his head. "Slocum, I'm too damn tired to even think about it. You?"

Slocum sighed. The temptation was strong. He had heard about a redhead who worked in Eddy, a woman who could do things that would damn near blow a man's balls into the next county. Then he thought of the bloody little bundle in his arms on the floor of a bank in Kansas and shook his head. The memory was still too fresh, too painful. "Guess I'll pass for now. I'm beginning to feel some of those miles myself."

8

Preacher Whiteside sat on a rocky outcrop overlooking the camp on the lower Pecos, his hands clenched into fists and pressed against his temples.

The voices were back.

The voices grew louder, a raging argument building inside his head as he moaned aloud. He rocked his body back and forth, eyes closed, trying to will the voices away, to banish them to the darkness and let him once again know peace. He had known the voices most of his life. One was evil, the words of the Prince of Darkness, reedy, whining; one righteous, the word of the Almighty, the thunderous bass tone a booming counterpoint to the other's wheedling. The evil voice seemed to come from below, at his feet. The righteous voice rumbled from the stars overhead. The two met and quarreled behind his eyebrows, sending agony raging through his skull.

"You have done well, Preacher," the voice of good thundered. "The Philistines have been punished for their sins. You have followed where I have led; now you must complete your mission."

"Not so, Eldon," said the wheedling voice, so hauntingly familiar, the first voice he remembered ever hearing. "The whore lives. The whore of Babylon. She must be destroyed."

"Preacher, hear me!" demanded the voice from above. "The girl is no whore! She is the virgin of Babylon and your passage to the promised land beyond the river Jordan!"

"Eldon, listen to me. The girl is no virgin." The high-pitched words hurt his ears. "There are no pure women, Eldon. Remember the smell, the taste of women? Remember how you were destroyed as a man? Remember the humiliation, the hurt, how you were cast out when you failed her? No woman should live to do such things to other men. Thou shalt not suffer a whore to live—"

"The dark one lies, Preacher!" The rage in the voice from above hammered into Whiteside's brain. Agony stabbed through the bridge of his nose. "I order you! Listen not to the words of the fallen one! Banish temptation! Your work for me is not finished! Beyond the river Jordan you will find peace; I will lead you to the green pastures, the still waters."

"Go away," Preacher whimpered. Tears trickled down his cheeks. "Leave me alone."

For a few heartbeats the voices fell silent. Then the reedy one returned: "They're following you, Eldon. Remember your promise—kill the whore!"

"No! I forbid it! Remember your vow, Preacher Whiteside! Smite only those who defile the Word! Punish them for their misdeeds! I will lead you to the sinners, so that you may send them before me for final judgment!"

"Why not send the whore to that judgment, Eldon? But first, give her to your men." The voice from below turned smooth and sly. "What better way to punish the whore than to give her a few moments to ply her trade? What better way to avenge the wrongs done you by those who follow?"

"Goddamn you both! You're tearing me apart!" Preacher Whiteside pressed his fists tighter about his temples. He knew the moment was near when his skull would explode and his brains scatter as if hit by a Sharps .50 slug. He pulled a fist away from his head and shook it toward the earth beneath his feet, then at the stars overhead. He pulled his pistol. "I won't give either of you the satisfaction!" He cocked the handgun and placed it against his right temple.

"No, Preacher! That is what the dark one wants! Would you spend eternity in the fires of hell?"

The muzzle of the gun in Preacher's hand wavered.

"Go ahead, Eldon," the other voice said, smooth and soothing. "Pull the trigger. We wait for you, we will welcome you, and your soul will be at peace."

The tremble in Preacher's hand grew to a shudder; he could feel the jittery tapping of the muzzle against his temple.

"Do not abandon me, Preacher!" The voice above boomed loud in Preacher's throbbing brain. "I can give you peace! Eternal rest! But first, you must complete your work in my name! Have I not sent more soldiers, to join you in less than a day's ride? Have I not promised even more warriors, a legion, beyond the river Jordan? Did I not choose you to lead this legion against the avarice and lust of the Philistines, making war upon them from a safe haven where no army dares tread? Think of the good your legion will do in my name. And think of this: Why does the dark one want your soul? It is because *she* is waiting for you there. Preacher Whiteside, I *forbid* you to commit the one unforgivable sin!"

An unseen hand seemed to grip Whiteside's wrist and pull the gun away. He watched, detached, as a thumb lowered the hammer. He thought it was his own thumb, but there was no feeling in his hand, only the raging agony in his head. The pistol slowly fell away and returned itself to his holster.

"Good, Preacher," the voice from above said. "You are a fine soldier. I will lead you to the end of your torment."

"They're following, Eldon." The voice from below was thin now, barely audible. "You will never reach the river Jordan while the whore lives—" The voice faded into the void of nothingness.

Preacher felt the sudden stab of pain low in his gut, as if his intestines were being torn from his body. He gagged. His stomach heaved. He retched and vomited, again and again, until only the pain of dry, wracking contractions remained. Gradually he regained his breath. The pain in his head had eased. He wiped a hand over the foul taste on his lips and sighed. The voices were gone. He smiled, secure once again in the knowledge that the Almighty rode at his side.

In the camp below, Victoria Tucker lay in her blankets, unable to sleep, despite the exhaustion of days on the trail and the constant fear of the unknown. The little .22 rimfire pistol pressed cold against her right knee from its hiding place deep inside the bedroll. It was a small comfort, and the constant worry over someone discovering it added to the tightness in Victoria's chest. But the cool touch of metal represented at least a hope. Without it, she would be completely helpless.

A few feet away the half-breed with the smoky eyes squatted by the fire, a tin coffee cup in his hand. He and Preacher had been her guards since the fight; Preacher now trusted neither Dade nor Jeb to keep watch over her.

Victoria wondered if Dirk Campbell ever slept. He seemed never to tire; the haunting gray eyes were always alert. Unlike the others, he was always clean-shaven. Perhaps his obvious Indian heritage bequeathed him little facial hair, she reasoned, but his clothing was somehow less soiled than that worn by the others, too. The expression in his eyes never seemed to change. There was no way to tell what the man felt or thought at any one time. He had been aloof but courteous to her ever since the raid on the bank. Yet there was an undercurrent of quiet violence about the man. She had heard the others say he was the best gunfighter in the group, fast and accurate with a pistol.

"Mr. Campbell?"

The half-breed turned to face her. "You should be asleep, Miss Tucker," he said softly. "You need to rest."

"I can't sleep. I keep thinking about—well, about Preacher." She sighed softly. "I see the way he looks at me. It's like he loathes the sight of me. I just don't understand—" Her voice trailed away.

Dirk Campbell stared at her for a moment, the expression in the gray eyes still unreadable. Then he half shrugged. "He's crazy. Hears voices."

Victoria fought a brief, losing battle against her curiosity. Besides, she reminded herself, the more she knew about her captors, the better her chance of making an escape. "Mr. Campbell, you've ridden with him for quite some time, haven't you?"

Campbell nodded. "Quite a few years."

"Then perhaps you can tell me. I see the way he looks at me, with complete loathing—like I was a pile of sheep droppings or something. Why does he hate me so?"

The half-breed was silent for a moment, as if trying to decide whether or not to answer. Then he sipped at the coffee, tossed the dregs from the cup onto the sand, and moved closer to her side.

"It's not just you, Miss Tucker. Preacher hates all women." Campbell glanced toward the rocky outcrop in the distance where the rail-thin figure sat, a faint silhouette against the blanket of stars. "I don't suppose it would hurt to tell you." He reached into a shirt pocket for his tobacco sack and began to roll a cigarette.

"It was his mother who scrambled Preacher's head. She was widowed shortly after he was born. His father was killed over a card game in some logging camp up North." He finished rolling the smoke and fired it with a twig from the small camp blaze. "She was a little crazy, too. Maybe a lot crazy. She wouldn't let Preacher out of the house much. Made him memorize the Bible for his schooling."

Campbell took another drag from the cigarette and let the smoke trickle from his nostrils. "Preacher was always mixed up, I think. But it was when he was about thirteen that she finished doing the job on his brain. She caught him in his room, playing with himself. She lit into him with a leather strap. Then she told him that if he was determined to sin, he might as well do it with a woman. With her."

"My God," Victoria muttered. "No wonder he despises women so."

Campbell stared at the cigarette in his fingers. "It got worse for him. She made Preacher share her bed, made him use tongue on her, made him service her like some stud horse most every night." Campbell took a final drag of the cigarette and tossed the butt into the fire. "One night, when Preacher was seventeen, eighteen years old, he couldn't get it up for her. She gave him a tongue lashing about what a sorry excuse of a man he was and beat him over the head with a Bible. Preacher killed her that night. Cut her open from crotch to chin with a butcher knife. By the time anyone found her, he was long gone for the high country, riding bareback on an old buggy horse."

Victoria swallowed against the taste of bile that had risen in her throat. "That—explains a lot, I guess." *It explains a lot more than you realize, mister,* she thought. "Why did you choose to ride with a madman like him?"

The half-breed shrugged. "He may be crazy, miss, but he's good at what he does. I've never been hungry or broke since I joined up with Preacher."

"And you'll stay with him?"

The smoke-colored eyes never changed expression. "I have nowhere else to go. This life's the only one I know. And it beats working sunup to sundown for a dollar a day."

Victoria fell silent, staring for a moment into the tiny flames that licked among the glowing coals of the small fire. "Mr. Campbell," she finally said, "what do you think Preacher will do with me?"

"That's anybody's guess, miss. If he's still in his righteous mood, he might keep his word and turn you loose. If he's not, who knows?"

Victoria cleared her throat. "And you, Mr. Campbell? Would you let him kill me, or worse, throw me to that animal Jeb Dawson?"

Dirk Campbell stared into her eyes. "Miss Tucker, I don't really give a damn what happens to you. But I do give a damn what happens to me. You're our ticket to Mexico. If we didn't have you along, we'd be up to our butts in lawmen before we made twenty miles. So until we cross the Rio Grande, I'll try to talk Preacher into keeping you alive. After that, who cares?"

The half-breed stood, strode back to his post at the fire, and rolled another cigarette. Victoria watched him go, then settled back onto her blankets, shaken more than she wanted to admit. She eased her hand into the bedroll, let her fingers touch the worn, smooth wooden grips of the little .22 pistol. *So there's no hope that the half-breed will help. But at least,* she swore silently, *I won't go without a fight—*

The sound of boots on sand interrupted the thought. She twisted her head as Preacher Whiteside walked unsteadily into the clearing. His face seemed pale, eyes bloodshot, brow wrinkled as if he were in pain. "Take over at the lookout, Dirk," he said, his voice shaky. "Be sober and vigilant, for the

Devil walks the night. I'll keep an eye on the child here."

Dirk stood and plucked his rifle from its rest across his saddle. "We'll have more soldiers soon, Dirk," Preacher said. "And the Almighty will lead us to fresh horses and supplies." Preacher waved toward the rocky outcrop where he had stood watch. A flicker of life returned to the pale blue eyes, grew until Whiteside's expression seemed almost joyful. "He came to me on the Mount of Olives, up there, and chased away the evil one. He has great plans for us, Dirk. As the Good Book says, 'Faith without His works is death; be ye doers of the world and not watchers.'"

Campbell merely nodded and strode away into the starlit night. Preacher Whiteside reached into Jeb Dawson's saddle-bag and retrieved a pint bottle of whiskey. "I must take communion now, child. The blood of the lamb soothes and restores the spirit." He tilted the bottle and drained half the contents without pausing for breath. Preacher sighed, wiped his lips, then lifted the bottle to his ear and shook it. He suddenly giggled, a high-pitched and girlish sound, and winked at Victoria. "The lamb must soon be bled some more, my young virgin. His blood is all but gone. This is the last of the sacrament." He lifted the bottle again, drained the contents, and slumped back against his saddle.

Moments later, Preacher Whiteside's resonant snores reverberated over the campsite. Victoria lay silent, unable to sleep. The stars overhead inched across the black sky, then finally winked out as the exhaustion of her body stilled the whirlwind of emotion in her mind.

Victoria came awake with a start at the touch on her shoulder. She almost cried out in alarm before a hand closed gently over her mouth.

"Be quiet, Victoria." It was Dade Fowler's whisper near her ear. "I have horses saddled. We only have one chance to get away. Move quickly, but keep it quiet."

Victoria slid from her blankets. It seemed to her that the pound of her heart against her ribs could wake the dead. She chanced a quick glance at Preacher Whiteside. The outlaw leader slumped against the saddle, snoring in a whiskey stupor.

She followed, placing each foot with care, as Fowler crept past Jeb Dawson's bedroll. The stocky man mumbled something and stirred; Victoria's breath caught in her throat. Then a soft, buzzing snore sounded from the blankets. Fowler waited for several heartbeats, then continued his careful stalk away from the camp to the shallow arroyo where the horses were picketed.

The first pale streak of the coming dawn sliced the eastern sky as Dade Fowler boosted her onto her horse, swung aboard his own mount, then leaned down to slash the picket ropes of the other horses in the outlaw band's small remuda.

Victoria's palms were slick with the cold sweat of raw terror as they rode at a slow walk toward the west, away from the breaking dawn. Her heart skidded as she remembered the .22 pistol still in her bedroll. In her haste and excitement she had forgotten the weapon.

Dade reined his mount close to hers. "Get ready to run for it," he said softly. "When we come out of this dry wash, Campbell will be able to see us from that lookout point. We've got to make the foothills of the Guadalupe Range before they catch us. There's no place to hide between here and there."

Victoria nodded. They rode in silence for a quarter of a mile before a yell sounded in the distant camp. Dade Fowler rammed spurs to his horse. "Ride!" he called.

Victoria slapped her bootheels against her horse's ribs, leaned forward to balance her weight on the stirrups, and felt the surge of powerful muscles beneath her. She realized for the first time that the horse she rode was not the slow pack mount. Dade had saddled Preacher's powerful bay for her. The horse's mane whipped against her hands as the two rode for their lives. She chanced a quick glance over her shoulder. The light was stronger now. In the distance two horsemen followed. One was the stocky Jeb Dawson, the second the tall man in the stovepipe hat. Dawson was a good hundred yards ahead of Preacher Whiteside.

Victoria's spirits surged. *We're going to make it,* she shouted to herself, *there's no way they can catch us now.* The rising sun touched the peaks of the Guadalupe mountains, beckoning to them like a lighthouse over the sea of rolling grasslands.

Dade Fowler suddenly barked a curse and yanked his horse to a sliding stop. Victoria hauled back on the reins; the bay skidded to a halt only a few feet from the edge of a deep, narrow wash carved into the plains by a creek. The sides of the small canyon were almost perpendicular, a sixty-foot drop to the floor of the unexpected gash in the earth.

"Dammit, this cut isn't supposed to be here," Fowler said. "I don't see a way down. We'll have to ride around!" He whirled his horse toward the approaching riders. "I don't see the half-breed!"

"Maybe he couldn't catch his horse," Victoria said.

"He had the horse with him." Fowler's face twisted in worry. "North. We'll have to ride north until we find a trail through this wash. Let's go!"

For almost a mile the two fugitives rode, urging tiring horses along the bank of the wash, dodging brush clumps and scrambling through shallow arroyos that fed the deeper wash below. They topped one rise and Dade Fowler jabbed a finger toward a narrow, sloping gash in the earth ahead.

"A trail down! We're going to make it, Victoria—"

A heavy, meaty sound like the slap of a hand on a quarter of beef cut off his words. Fowler seemed to rise from the saddle, yanked upward by some unknown harness. Victoria cried out as the sound of a big-bore rifle slammed through the dawn. Fowler fell heavily, rolled in the rocky soil, and lay crumpled against a small juniper.

Victoria instinctively checked her mount. "Dade!" she called, her voice cracking in shock and fear. Then she started to rein her horse about—and felt the animal stagger as the hand slapped the beef again. She kicked free of the stirrups as the horse went down. The ground slammed into her side. She lay, unable to breathe, the air knocked from her lungs, as the echoes of the second rifle shot rumbled down the steep wash. The sky darkened and went black.

Victoria fought her way back to consciousness. She heard the sound of hoofbeats approaching and tried to get to her feet, to find a place to hide. Her legs refused to work. Then she was staring into the scarred face of Jeb Dawson, a smirk of triumph slashing the leathery skin. She tried to scramble away on hands and knees. A heavy fist clamped against her shoulder and spun her onto her back.

"Now I've got you, you little bitch," Dawson muttered. The big hand closed on Victoria's shirt collar and yanked. The cloth ripped; she grabbed Dawson's forearm, tried to push it away, swung a feeble fist at his face. The fall had drained all the strength from her. Victoria felt the chill morning air on her exposed breasts.

Dawson roughly shoved her back and stood over her. He reached for the waistband of her pants with his right hand and fumbled with the buttons of his trousers with his left. "By God, I've been waitin' long enough for a piece of you, you little bitch—and now I'm goin' to get it!" Spittle dribbled from the corner of his mouth.

Victoria forced back a wave of revulsion and tried to bring herself to accept her fate. She closed her eyes, unable to bring to herself to watch. It would be brutal, she knew. She could only hope it would be quick, and that she would still be alive when it was over.

She felt her trousers yanked down, stripped over her boots, and cast aside. Rough hands grabbed the insides of her knees, started to force her legs apart—and abruptly stopped.

"Far enough, Jeb." Dirk Campbell's voice was soft but deadly. Victoria opened her eyes. Jeb Dawson knelt before her, pants stripped down to his ankles, his body streaked with filth and sweat. The muzzle of Dirk Campbell's rifle rested against the side of Dawson's head.

"What the hell you doin', you damn half-breed?" Dawson's challenge was tempered by a touch of fear and uncertainty.

"I'm going to blow your brains over forty acres if you don't get away from the girl," Campbell said.

Dawson's face flushed in rage. "You want her for yourself, you son of a bitch?"

"No. It's your choice, Dawson. Won't hurt my feelings a bit to pull this trigger. I don't like you much, anyway. You think with your prick instead of your brains, and you're not all that well equipped in either department."

Dawson's face went livid. He cursed and raged and threatened both Campbell and Victoria, but he was pulling up his pants in the meantime. Victoria crabbed away from the swarthy man, dragging her clothes, and when she was safely out of reach, dressed as rapidly as she could. The shirt was all but ruined. It no longer covered all of her breasts.

The whole incident had taken only moments. By the time Preacher Whiteside rode up on the slow-footed, winded pack horse, Campbell had lowered the rifle.

The tall man glanced at the dead horse, at Dade Fowler's crumpled body by the juniper, then glared at the trio dismounted before him. "What happened, Dirk?"

The half-breed shrugged. "I guessed right. When they hit this canyon, they turned north. Rode right into my sights."

"You killed my best horse, Dirk."

"It was either that or the girl. I figured we needed her more than the horse."

"And you, Dawson?"

Jeb Dawson swallowed. He glanced at Dirk Campbell. "It was—all over when I got here," he said lamely.

"The girl's clothes?"

"Torn when the horse went down," Campbell said calmly.

"Cover yourself, young woman," Preacher said. His voice held an ominous tone. "You broke a solemn vow, girl. You promised you wouldn't try to escape."

Victoria did not reply. There was nothing she could say. She tugged at the torn shirt, trying to hold it together.

"I should kill you for this," Preacher Whiteside said.

"I wouldn't do that, Preacher," Campbell interrupted. "As long as we've got her, nobody will try to jump us."

Preacher's brow furrowed in thought. It seemed to Victoria that his brain must still be hazy from the whiskey. Finally, he shrugged. "You're right, Dirk. We need the virgin." He glared at Victoria. "For now we follow the Book of Peter: 'Charity covers the sins of the multitudes.'" He jabbed a finger toward Jeb Dawson. "And you, Dawson, heed these words from the same disciple: 'Abstain from fleshly lust lest ye be cursed to damnation.' Boost the girl up behind me, Dirk. We've lost time. More soldiers await us at Pope's Crossing. In a vision last night, the Almighty showed me a place where we will find horses and supplies, and beyond that are the waters of the river Jordan, where we will form our legion."

"What about our young friend Fowler?"

"Leave him. The flesh of traitors is nothing more than food for jackals."

Slocum reined his mount to a stop on a low ridge overlooking a broad, grassy valley south of the Pecos River. An isolated ranch house stood a half mile below in the bend of a small creek choked with wild berry thickets and a stand of stunted junipers.

"What is it, Slocum?"

"Buzzards circling over the house," Slocum said, his voice cold. "No smoke from the chimney, and it's near suppertime. No horses in the corral. The Whiteside gang's tracks lead straight toward it."

Slocum heard the whisper of metal against leather as Link drew his .45-90 Winchester from the saddle boot. "You think they're still down there?"

"I doubt it," Slocum replied. "There's no sign of life. Buzzards wouldn't be landing if there were people around. And the tracks we've been following are a day old, at least." He heard the touch of disgust in his own voice. They hadn't been able to gain ground on Whiteside despite pushing their horses almost to the limits of endurance.

They had been a day late at the deep arroyo across from the Sacramentos. The coyotes and buzzards hadn't left much of the young man they'd found dead there, but the tracks were clear enough. The dead man and Victoria had tried to make a run for it. The man paid with his life, and Whiteside still had Victoria. They had been a day late at Pope's Crossing, too. Whiteside now had three new guns in his bunch. *We're getting nowhere awful damn fast,* Slocum thought, *and I don't like the looks of this at all.*

"We'd best check it out, Link." Slocum levered a round into the chamber of his Winchester. "Watch yourself. We don't want any surprises. We'll ride in from the northwest and come up behind the barn. You hang back, follow at about fifty yards or so. If there is anybody down there, they won't get an easy shot at both of us that way."

Slocum nudged his horse into a slow walk, circling the house until he reached the creek. The berry vines were too dense for passage, the junipers too short to conceal a man on horseback. Slocum felt more than a little naked as he rode toward the house, rifle at the ready. The crude pole gate of the corral was down; the back door of the house stood open, sagging on one torn hinge. An ax leaned against the woodpile, a stack of kindling nearby. The outhouse door stood ajar, the scent of its recent use sharp in Slocum's nostrils.

He dismounted at the west wall of the house and eased his way toward the front, stalking the squawks of feeding buzzards. Other birds wheeled overhead; one soared in to land, spotted Slocum, and banked sharply away, ponderous wings flapping in the still air.

Slocum peered around the side of the house. One quick glance told him what the buzzards were eating. The bodies of two men lay crumpled a few feet from the front porch. Slocum waited, listening and sniffing the air, until he was satisfied no ambush lay ahead, then rounded the corner.

Both the men wore coarse coveralls now dark with dried blood. One was past middle age, the other a few years younger. Both had been shot several times. Slocum eased away from the bodies to the front door. It also stood open.

"Anybody home? Hello, the house," Slocum called.

There was no answer. He stepped through the door. Inside, the house was a shambles. Pantry doors stood open, papers littered the floor, the cookstove lay on its side. The covers had been stripped from the two beds in adjoining rooms and the mattresses slashed open. Feathers and ticking swirled around Slocum's boots as he backed from the second bedroom. He found nothing of value, no food, guns, or ammunition in the house. Whiteside's bunch had stripped it to the bone. The only thing that seemed undisturbed was the lace curtain over one front window.

Slocum stepped outside and waved to Link. The young man kneed his horse into a slow trot toward the house. At the corner of his vision Slocum glimpsed a movement in the dense berry thicket.

"Watch it, Link!" he yelled. "Something at the creek!"

Link immediately swung down on the offside, putting the horse's body between himself and the creek, his rifle barrel across the saddle seat. Slocum sprinted from the porch and ran to the thicket a few yards south of the point where he had spotted the movement. He reached the sharp-thorned tangle of bushes and vines, paused to catch his breath, and began a careful stalk toward the spot where he had seen the flash of movement. It could be nothing—a coyote, maybe, or a calf— but a man who took chances in spots like this didn't live long enough to find out if he was wrong.

Slocum stalked patiently, pausing every other step to watch and listen. He glanced once toward Link and saw that he had taken up a position behind a thick corner post of the corral, ready to provide covering fire if needed.

A faint scrape of cloth against thorn only a few feet away reached Slocum's ears. He crouched, peered through a small opening at the base of a wild berry vine, and saw a patch of checkered cloth. He lined the muzzle of his rifle on the spot. "Show yourself or I'll shoot," he called.

The spot of cloth moved, rustled, and a moment later Slocum felt his jaw drop in surprise as a woman crawled through a small opening in the brush. She stood and stared at Slocum, her hazel eyes wide with the look of a frightened doe, yet somehow strong and defiant. Tangled auburn hair flecked with dried leaves and debris fell to her shoulders. The checkered housedress she wore was torn almost to rags; it did nothing to conceal her high, firm breasts or slim waist. A tear along one side revealed a scratched and dirty but smoothly muscled and shapely thigh. Trim ankles topped a pair of what appeared to be heavy men's shoes, the type favored by farmers.

"Who are you? Are you one of them?" The voice was wary, frightened.

"Easy, miss," Slocum said. He lowered the rifle. "I mean you no harm. Are you hurt?"

The wariness in the deep hazel eyes faded slightly. "I haven't been injured. Who are you?"

"My name is Slocum. I'm tracking some men. It looks like they've been here. They're led by a tall man who wears a frock coat and a stovepipe hat."

"They were the ones." The hazel eyes were calm, with no hint of tears or pain. "They killed my husband and his brother. For no real reason. Just shot them down like mad dogs." She wavered on her feet, looked as if she were going to collapse.

Slocum was at her side in two strides. She sagged against him. He felt the warmth of her body on his flesh as he slipped an arm around her waist. "Are you sure you're all right, ma'am?"

She nodded. The sun painted reddish-gold highlights in the tangle of thick auburn hair. "I'm—all right—just so thirsty— no water in the creek."

"We'll get you some water, ma'am," Slocum said gently. "Don't worry now. You're safe." He started to lead her to the front of the house, remembered the bodies in the yard, and abruptly changed directions. He supported most of her weight as he steered her to the rear of the house where a stone-walled well stood.

She stiffened as Link strode up, his brows raised in question. "Link's with me, ma'am," Slocum said. She sagged against the stones until Slocum hauled up a wooden bucket and filled a tin dipper. She pulled herself erect, grabbed the dipper, and drank the contents without stopping.

"Take it easy," Slocum cautioned. "Not too much at one time. When you feel up to it, tell me what happened."

He let her have another dipper of water. She sat on the edge of the stone well as she drank. Slocum noted with satisfaction that this time she didn't gulp the water down, but sipped it.

"They came this morning," she said. "Five or six men. I was down in the thicket, gathering berries for a cobbler I was going to cook. They never saw me. They hailed the house. When my husband went out, they shot him." Her voice trembled slightly. A slight shudder rippled her body.

Slocum put a reassuring hand on her arm. "Take your time. I'm sorry about your loss." He waited until she seemed to regain her composure. Up close, Slocum noted, beneath the dirt, welts, and scratches from the berry vines, she was a fine figure of a woman. She had the sort of profile seen on ivory brooches, but with slightly higher cheekbones and a firm, almost square, jawline. She wore no corset; a whisper of wind flared the torn housedress, momentarily exposing a startlingly full breast tipped by a dark circle of pigment almost the size of a half dollar. She didn't seem aware of the flash of skin. Slocum swallowed. He knew he was letting his attention drift from the problem at hand. "What's your name?"

"Edna. Edna Dellafield."

Slocum pulled a clean kerchief from a hip pocket, moistened it with a dribble of well water, and dabbed at a scratch oozing blood along her forearm. He glanced at Link. The young man seemed rooted in place, unsure of what to do or say. "Link, fetch that bottle of barber's alcohol from my saddlebag. Then see if you can find a shovel. We've got a couple of men to bury."

Link nodded, apparently relieved at having some chores to tend. "Mrs. Dellafield, did you see those men well enough to describe them to me?" Slocum asked.

Edna Dellafield nodded. "The tall one in the top hat stayed off to one side. There was a small person with him. A young boy, or maybe a girl, hands tied and a rope around the neck. The tall one held the other end of the rope."

Link returned with the bottle. Slocum dribbled a bit of the liquid onto the kerchief. "This may sting a little bit," he said, "but we don't want those scratches to get infected. Now, about the others?"

She winced as he dabbed at a scratch on her shoulder. Slocum nodded as she described the gang. It sounded to him like Stony Lollar, Jesus Quintana, and Jeb Dawson had done the shooting while Buck Teague and the half-breed, Dirk Campbell, sacked the house and stole the horses. *So now we know we're up against at least five men, all of them top gunhands,* Slocum thought, *and now we've got to do something about this woman.* He heard the sound of metal against sand from the front of the house. Link had wasted no time finding a shovel and starting a grave.

Slocum nodded as Edna Dellafield ended her account of the attack. "Those are the men we're after, all right." He paused for a moment, not sure if he should clean the scratches on some of the more feminine portions of her anatomy. "Do you have friends or family nearby? Someplace where we could take you?"

She shook her head. Slocum eyed a scratch along one shapely thigh, decided it was no time for chivalry, and dabbed at the cut. "I have no one," she said. "This was to be my home. It's gone now. I can't stay here."

"No, ma'am," Slocum said, "you can't." He swabbed at a scratch on the side of her left breast and decided he was beginning to enjoy the chore a little too much. He handed her the bottle and the kerchief. "I'd best go lend Link a hand with the graves," he said.

The sun had set before Slocum and Link laid the Dellafield brothers to rest—with no tears from the new widow, Slocum noticed—and fixed a simple supper. They tended their horses and spread bedrolls on the front porch. Slocum had helped Edna Dellafield find enough ticking and blankets for a makeshift bed inside. Now he sat on his roll, smoking a cigarillo, and stared off toward the southwest. Miles away the last of the light began to fade over the Davis Mountains. Miles that they had yet to cover before they caught up with Whiteside's gang. And now the gang had fresh horses. It was beginning to look like Whiteside would beat them to Helltown, Slocum thought.

"Slocum?"

"Yes, Link?"

"What do we do with the woman?"

Slocum sighed. "We have to take her along, at least for a while. She and I had a talk about it. She has no friends, no family, no money. We can't leave her here to starve or at the mercy of some bunch like Whiteside's, and there are a lot of those types in this country."

"She'll slow us down, Slocum."

Slocum took a drag from the cigarillo and grinned at Link. "That's what I thought about you at first, friend," he said.

9

Texans had a saying that Presidio was the place the Devil came to warm up when it got to be winter in hell.

Slocum swabbed the sweat from his face and conceded the Texans were right. By day the ancient cluster of adobe buildings on the bank of the Rio Grande broiled under the high sun, with temperatures climbing into triple figures. By night it didn't cool off a hell of a lot either, Slocum mused.

And just fifteen miles away, in the place called Helltown, it was going to get a lot hotter.

Slocum lay naked on the too-soft feather bed in the boarding-house on the south side of the plaza, his Colt and the last bottle of Old Overholt on the rickety table beside the oversized cot. An oil lamp flickered a weak gold wash over the room. When the time for sleep came, Slocum would douse the lamp, open the shutters on the lone window, and hope for a passing breeze to ease the stifling heat.

The ride from the Dellafield place had been brutal. Sixteen hours a day in the saddle on the Helltown Trail that wound through the Davis Mountains and the cactus-studded wasteland called Mustang Desert had taken its toll on both people and horses. It had been worse on the horses.

Slocum was accustomed to long, hard rides. It was part of his way of life. Link had also become toughened to the trail. His face was now sunbrowned and lined from wind and weather, and he had shown a capacity for endurance that surprised Slocum. Link still had a spring in his step and the eager look of a stalking mountain cat in those strange amber eyes.

Edna Dellafield had also surprised Slocum. She had endured the torturous hours, thirst, heat, and slim camp rations without a whimper. She had salvaged a change of clothing from the wreckage of her home, and rode a makeshift Indian-style blanket saddle on Link's pack mount. And she was a good hand with a horse. She knew when to let the animal have its head, when to take charge, and she rode with a fine sense of balance. She was as steady in the head as she was in the saddle; she quickly banished the initial shock of the attack and the death and violence it brought. Instead of starting at shadows and whimpering in self-pity as many women would under the circumstances, Edna Dellafield rode with a quiet confidence and self-assurance.

Slocum had learned a lot about Edna Dellafield on the long days on the trail to Presidio—and the more he learned, the more he liked what he saw. Mrs. Dellafield was more than just tough. She was bright, with a quick mind, and was well educated. She had, she freely admitted, made one major mistake in her life. The mistake was Mr. Dellafield. She had married him after a brief courtship in East Texas, believing his lies about his riches and land holdings, and they had moved out West to begin a new life.

The late Mr. Dellafield had proved to be as much a disappointment to her as a husband as his claims were empty. That was why she had shed no tears over his grave. She was, she said, not burying a husband, but burying her biggest error in judgment.

Above all, Slocum knew he was in the presence of a woman. He felt the tension between them, a tension they both tried to deny by carrying respect and courtesy to the extreme. The look in her eye and the way she carried her body reminded Slocum of a caged tigress he had seen in a traveling circus once. A man who opened that cage did so at his own risk. Or possibly, Slocum mused, his own pleasure.

A hesitant tap at the door jarred Slocum from his reverie.

He lifted the Peacemaker from the bedside table, cocked the weapon, and almost as an afterthought flipped the coarse muslin sheet over his lower body.

"Come in," Slocum called.

The door swung open and Edna Dellafield stepped into the room. The weak light of the oil lamp played against the folds of the oversized man's shirt she wore in place of a nightgown. The shirt ended just above her knees. It did little to hide the swell of well-formed breasts. Slocum lowered the hammer and replaced the pistol on the table.

"I hope I'm not disturbing you, Mr. Slocum," she said, leaning her back against the door. "I know it's late, but I couldn't sleep. The heat—" Her voice trailed away as she brushed a damp tendril of auburn hair from her forehead.

"You're not bothering me at all, Mrs. Dellafield," Slocum said. That was a bare-assed lie, Slocum told himself. He could already feel the tension begin to build in his crotch. "I'm having a bit of trouble getting to sleep, myself. Something you would like to talk about?"

She strode to the bed and sat on the edge of the mattress, facing Slocum. The motion pulled the nightshirt high up one thigh, exposing a substantial swatch of smooth skin, white except for the dark lines of healing scratches.

"Mr. Slocum, I'll get right to the point," Edna said. "I think I can be honest with you." Her gaze was steady and calm on Slocum's face. "I'm no good at being coy, and I'm lousy at playing games." There was a quiet intensity in the contralto voice. "If I seem too forward, or if I offend you, just say so and I'll leave, no questions asked or feelings hurt."

"I don't offend easily, Mrs. Dellafield," Slocum said, "especially when a beautiful woman comes calling. Provided she isn't holding a shotgun."

Edna Dellafield chuckled aloud, a soft, musical sound from deep in her throat. "I assure you, sir, that I am unarmed. And I thank you for the compliment." The smile faded from full lips. "Mr. Slocum, I have been—or I was—married for eighteen months. For the last year of that marriage my husband never touched me." She lowered her gaze briefly, her face flushed. "Celibacy has never been one of my favorite states, Mr. Slocum. I need a man But not just any man. I need you."

Slocum felt his heartbeat quicken. He knew where it was pumping the blood. So did Edna Dellafield. She reached out and lay a warm palm over the swelling in the sheet at his groin. "I'm no whore, Mr. Slocum," she said, gently stroking his erection, "but I know what I want and morality be damned. I'll ask for it."

"No need to ask twice in this room, Mrs. Dellafield," Slocum said. He put a hand on her thigh. The skin was smooth and warm, the muscles firm. He let his hand slip higher. Edna Dellafield leaned her head back and moaned, eyes closed, as Slocum's hand touched the dense thicket of hair at the junction of her legs. He stroked her pubic hair gently, then let his fingers slip between her legs. She opened her thighs to his touch; her breath came more rapidly as he explored the warm, moist lips with gentle fingers. She moaned again, softly, then shivered.

Abruptly, she stood, stripped the nightshirt over her head, tossed the sheet from Slocum's body, and lay beside him on the bed. Slocum's hand stroked the soft, pliable flesh of her breasts and toyed with the erect nipples as he lowered his head and kissed her. Her full lips parted, her tongue flicking against his, as she drew him to her. Her hand drifted to Slocum's groin, stroked the tight skin over his testicles, and closed around his shaft. She spread her thighs wide and guided him into her, eyes closed. her breath seemed to catch in her throat as Slocum slowly penetrated her. He lay still for a moment, savoring the feel of the snug, moist heat inside her. He cupped a hand to her breast, lowered his head, and ran his tongue around her nipple. The rise and fall of her chest quickened; she moaned aloud. Her hips moved, thrusting him even deeper into her, then drew back. Slocum's hips moved in response to hers, slowly at first, then more quickly. It seemed to Slocum that only a few seconds had passed before she cried out, her muscles convulsed, and she buried her head in his shoulder. Deep shudders wracked her body. Long, strong legs clamped hard over his buttocks, holding him deep inside, until the contractions against his shaft began to ease. Slocum felt the pressure build in his scrotum. He brought the full weight of his concentration to bear, held back the impending ejaculation, unwilling to end the intense pleasure of their coupling. After a moment, he heard her low moans begin once more; her pelvis moved, thrusting, pulling him into her, and then her muscles contracted once again. She gasped aloud in the throes of orgasm. Slocum could hold back no longer. He exploded into her, his jaws clenched as the powerful contractions turned his body rigid. For what seemed to be an eternity, he felt his shaft jerk and throb, answered by her own pulsations. Finally, he was spent, his body covered with perspiration, their skin slippery with sweat where they touched.

Slocum slowly became aware that he was resting too much of his weight on her. He lifted his torso with his elbows and smiled down at her. Edna Dellafield's arms fell away from his shoulders and dropped, limp, at her side. Slocum noticed that there were tears in her eyes and a streak of moisture down her cheeks. He wiped them away with a thumb.

She blinked up at him, her eyes languid, facial muscles relaxed. She smiled in wistful relief. "Mr. Slocum," she said, "you are a work of art."

Slocum chuckled and winked. "And you, Mrs. Dellafield, have just disconnected every joint in my body. I may never walk again, and it's all your fault, woman."

She traced a finger along his jawline. "Thank you, Mr. Slocum."

Slocum raised his eyebrows in mock surprise. "*You* are thanking *me*? It should be the other way around."

"So we thank each other," she said. "Now, sir, please remove your sweaty body from atop me. I am finished with you. For the time being, at least."

Slocum rolled aside and stared up at the ceiling for a moment. He hadn't felt so relaxed and content in days.

"Mr. Slocum, do you think I'm a slut?"

"Not in the least," he answered honestly. "I think you're a remarkable woman, Mrs. Dellafield. In many ways." He reached for a cigarillo from the nightstand.

"May I have one of those?"

The question startled Slocum for a moment. He had met a few women who smoked cigars. Most of them fell a bit short of Edna Dellafield's class. He handed her one of the thin tubes of tobacco, scratched a match, and lit both smokes. The two lay in contented silence for a moment.

"What happens now, Mr. Slocum? With the Whiteside gang, I mean."

Slocum sighed. He let go of the warmth and comfort of the moment with reluctance. "Link and I ride into Helltown tomorrow," he said thoughtfully, "and see if we can find the girl. Then try to figure out some way to get her out alive."

"It won't be easy, will it?"

"No. It will be damned tough. Whiteside will be surrounded by guns now. He has five of his own men, and only God knows how many others will back him."

"Do those men in Helltown know you or Link?"

"Some of them will know me, probably," Slocum said wryly. "I've crossed paths with a number of unsavory types over the years. Jesus Quintana knows me damned well. I put a slug in him once." Slocum took a long, thoughtful drag at the smoke. "I don't know if they would recognize Link. It depends on whether they saw him before they hit the bank in Scott's Ford. Any holdup man worth his own sweat would scout a town and its bank mighty well before making a move. Preacher Whiteside may be crazy as a loon, but he's good at his work."

The two smoked in silence for a time. Finally, Edna Dellafield leaned across Slocum's body and stubbed her cigarillo out in a stone ashtray on the bedside table. "They don't know me," she said. "None of them saw me during the raid on my place. Maybe I can help."

Slocum glanced at her, alarmed. "No. I want you to stay here in Presidio where you'll be safe. My God, woman, you could get killed in that place! Or worse!"

Edna Dellafield yawned and stretched. "Anybody could get killed there. But I think I'd be safe enough. Not even outlaws would dare harm a woman. At least not an outwardly decent one."

"This bunch might." Slocum's tone was as near to pleading as it ever got.

"Slocum, I *want* to help. You and Link came to my aid. I would have died by now without you two. And I want to help that poor girl. Tomorrow morning, rent me a buggy and buy a shotgun. A twenty-gauge, with short barrels, if you can find one. I've got a plan in mind."

"Edna, I won't hear of it!"

"Yes you will, Slocum." She grinned at him. "And thanks for using my first name. I think we can forget about being so formal, under the circumstances. In the meantime, I think I can get to sleep now. I haven't been so relaxed in months. You should rest, too. We'll argue about it in the morning."

She snuggled against his shoulder. Within moments, her breathing was deep and regular. Despite the oppressive heat, Slocum made no attempt to move away from her. *This is one dangerous woman to a man like me,* he thought. *I could get used to her mighty quick.*

The lamp guttered out, its fuel consumed. Slocum closed his eyes. He fell asleep with the sound of Edna's breathing in his ear and the scent of her in his nostrils.

Victoria Tucker huddled in a corner of the main room in the sprawling adobe building on the outskirts of the motley collection of structures that made up the outlaw stronghold of Helltown. Ropes bound her wrists and ankles, and a thin rawhide riata scratched at the skin of her throat, the free end attached to an iron ring on the wall. The failed escape attempt had ended what scant freedom she had been granted in the early days of her captivity.

The stifling heat inside the closed room compounded her misery. Sweat stung the abrasions where the rope had chafed her skin. But now she hardly noticed the pain. Raw fear had pushed it aside.

A few feet away, near the front door, the tall man in the top hat and frock coat sat in a straight-backed rawhide chair, his hands pressed against his temples. His leathery face twisted in agony. His body rocked back and forth; low moans and an occasional slurred shout issued from his throat.

"No, damn you!" The voice seemed to come from beyond instead of from the thin man's narrow chest. "Be gone! Leave me in peace! Have you not caused me enough pain? Release me, damn your soul!"

Victoria watched in fascination and growing terror as Preacher Whiteside hunched forward, arms clasped about his midsection, and shuddered violently. He suddenly bolted from the chair and dashed out the front door. Seconds later, Victoria heard the sounds of violent retching from beyond the doorway. Her own stomach churned in reflex at the obscene sound. She swallowed against the bile rising in her throat and drew several deep breaths of the close, heavy air in the room.

She started, her muscles tensed, as the tall man strode back into the room, wiping a trace of vomit from the stubble on his chin. He stood erect, narrow shoulders no longer slumped. Rage flashed in his almost colorless eyes as he swept the top hat from his head and flung it into a corner, then ripped the frock coat from his body and hurled it aside. He stood for a moment and stared at her, his face contorted in fury. He did not speak.

"Preacher," Victoria said, her voice shaky, "what's wrong? Are you sick?"

The rage drained from the weathered face, and a puzzled expression took its place. "Preacher? Why did you call me that? Preacher's gone."

"Gone?"

"My name is Eldon." The voice tightened as anger returned. "Don't call me Preacher. That man is crazy. He hears voices."

"I—I don't understand," Victoria stammered.

Whiteside glared at her. "It's not for you to understand, you little slut. Now that Preacher's gone, I've got to figure out what the hell to do with you."

"But you—he—Preacher. He promised to release me. After we reached this place." Victoria heard the growing desperation in her voice. Fear fed the rivulets of sweat that trickled down her body. "Don't you remember the promise?"

Whiteside wiped a bony hand across a sweat-beaded brow. "A promise from a crazy man? Why should I remember that, or give a damn?" A pleased expression gleamed in Whiteside's wild eyes. "Preacher didn't mention any promises before he left. But he did leave me a plan, an idea that will make me a rich man." Whiteside rubbed his hands together in pleased anticipation. "A magnificent idea. I wish I had thought of it myself: the greatest raiding party of all time."

Whiteside began to pace the length of the room, his long hands fluttering in growing excitement. "First, the silver shipments from the Mimbres Mountain mines. Use that money to fund a raid on the richest bank in El Paso." He slammed a doubled fist into an open palm. "And finally, the greatest of all robberies: the entire army payroll for forts Hood and Concho!" The tall man stopped his pacing and stared into space for a moment. "I'll need lots of men—" He suddenly glanced around, then whirled to face Victoria. "Men—where are my men?"

Victoria cleared her throat nervously. "Preacher gave them money. He told them to 'tree the town,' get their hell-raising and womanizing and drinking over with. That he didn't expect them back until tomorrow night."

Whiteside shook his head in disgust and resignation. "That sounds like Preacher. He never had my eye for detail. No matter. I have plans to make." He started pacing again, his footsteps raising puffs of dust on the dirt floor. "The men won't be a problem. That's what brought Preacher to Helltown in the first place. But the money—I *must* have more money—" Whiteside suddenly paused in his pacing and stared at Victoria. "You. That's why Preacher brought you."

Victoria squirmed under his steady gaze. "I—I don't understand. He promised to let me go."

"He lied. He brought you to raise money for the expedition!" Whiteside cackled in delight. "Maybe Preacher isn't so crazy after all."

"What do you plan to do with me?"

"Simple, young woman. I'm going to let you raise the money for my raid." He came closer, let his gaze drift over her huddled body. "Under that dirt and those worn-out clothes is a woman's body," he said. "Tomorrow night we'll get you cleaned up, buy you a new dress, and then I'll put you on the auction block. Sell you to the highest bidder. Then again to the next highest, and so on until we've taken the last half dollar in Helltown."

• • •

Slocum waited in a dry wash four miles outside of Helltown and glanced at the sun for the dozenth time in the last two hours. He had wanted to ride on into the outlaw stronghold at Edna Dellafield's side. Stopping the escort here made sense, maybe, but it didn't stop the worm of worry that writhed in his gut.

"Relax, Slocum," Link said at his side. "Blinding yourself looking at the sun won't make the time pass faster."

Slocum cocked an eyebrow at Link. "You don't look so damn relaxed yourself."

Link's expression was grim. Worry and anger flickered alternately in the amber eyes. "I'm not," he said, his voice taut, "but there's nothing we can do until Mrs. Dellafield gets back. Slocum, you've been nagging me since Scott's Ford to be patient. Now take your own advice. This is no time to get antsy and do something dumb."

Slocum drew in a deep breath of the scorching northern Chihuahua desert air. *The kid's right again,* Slocum thought. *Make a mistake now and I could get all four of us killed.* He snorted the dust from his nostrils.

"Link, if anything happens to Edna—" Slocum's voice trailed away. He wasn't sure how to finish the statement.

"I know, Slocum. I've been thinking the same thing about Victoria all the way from Kansas." Link dropped a hand to the butt of the .45 at his side. "If it means anything, I'll promise you this: If either of the women are hurt, you and I will make damn sure every one of those bastards pays, and pays hard."

Slocum turned his head to study Link's face. The young man's jaw was set in determination. The expression in the amber eyes was cold and deliberate. *I've got to quit calling this youngster son,* Slocum told himself. *He's damn sure a man grown now—a Western man who's earned his spurs.* He nodded. "That we will, Link. That we will."

It seemed to Slocum that the afternoon had no end. The sun broiled down on the waiting horsemen; there was little shade in the rocky arroyo, only an occasional clump of sage, bear grass, or cactus, barely enough to shelter a jackrabbit. The horses grew edgy with thirst and the aggravation of the swarms of heel flies that tormented them constantly. Still they waited, two men staring down a narrow, dusty road leading to the most lawless place on the face of the earth.

Finally, Slocum saw a plume of dust rising along the trail to Helltown. He sighed in relief as the tiny black spot at the head of the plume took shape. It was a buggy.

"Looks like it's time to mount up, Slocum," Link said. Slocum heard the faint touch of anxiety in the young man's tone. Slocum knew the feeling. It had crawled along his own spine many times over the years.

They met Edna Dellafield at the shallow crossing of the dry wash. The emerald-green dress she wore was coated with dust, her hair had come loose from the bun at the base of her neck and fell in tangles over her shoulders, and streaks of sweat painted white stripes through the dirt on her face. To Slocum, she was one beautiful sight. He dismounted at the side of the buggy, reached in and placed a welcoming hand on her forearm. "Any trouble, Edna?"

Edna smiled and shook her head. "Nothing serious. A few propositions, but no real threats. You know, Slocum, I could have made over a hundred dollars down there today." She chuckled, the resonance deep in her throat, and patted the stock of the sawed-off twenty-gauge at her side. "I never even had to pull this thing." Her smile faded. "I found out where Victoria is, Slocum," she said. "It's not good. The damn building they're holding her in is a fortress."

Slocum frowned. He had hoped it might be easier. "Can we get her out safely?"

The expression in Edna's eyes turned grim. "With luck, maybe. But we can't do anything tonight." She lifted the reins. "Let's get on back to Presidio, tend the horses, and make our war plans," she said.

"Mrs. Dellafield," Link interrupted, "is Victoria all right?"

"For the moment, yes." Edna's expression softened as she gazed at the young man.

"What do you mean by that? For the moment?"

"Link, they're going to auction her off tomorrow night. To the highest bidders, one at a time."

Link winced as if slapped in the face. His jaw went slack in momentary disbelief. Then the stunned look in the amber eyes gave way to growing fury. "Those dirty sons of bitches! Let's go, Slocum," he snapped. He started to rein his horse toward Helltown.

Slocum reached out and grabbed the headstall of the bridle on Link's horse. "Easy, Link. We've got to have a plan. If we go charging in there blind, all we'll get is killed. That wouldn't help Victoria."

"Let go of the bridle, Slocum."

"Not until you calm down," Slocum said. "We're going to have to plan this like it was a military campaign. We're only going to get one chance at it, Link. Don't get crazy on me now."

The rage and hurt slowly faded from Link's face. His shoulders slumped in resignation. "All right, Slocum. You don't have to chew my butt again about being patient. We'll play it your way."

Slocum hunched over the small table in Edna's room in the Presidio hotel and studied the sketch she had drawn on a sheet of paper. What he saw didn't look promising.

The sprawling adobe where Victoria was held prisoner stood on the outskirts of Helltown at the end of a narrow strip of sand that was the settlement's main street. The trail leading into town cut through a narrow notch in a low ridge that ran roughly north to south almost three hundred yards from the adobe. The building stood alone, separated from other structures by at least twenty yards. The ridges flanking the cut provided the only natural cover.

Edna said it appeared there was one room in the house that had no windows. Logic told Slocum that Victoria would be in that room. To reach her they would have to run a gauntlet of guns if they tried a simple assault.

The adobe walls were thick enough to blunt a howitzer shell, let alone stop a rifle slug. Narrow windows along all four walls gave those inside a commanding field of fire. Any kind of outright attack would give Preacher Whiteside time to kill Victoria. There was no doubt in Slocum's mind that the madman would do precisely that.

"I told you it was a fortress, Slocum," Edna said. She stared at the sketch and sighed. "On the surface, it looks impossible."

Slocum glanced at the auburn-haired woman and shook his head. "Nothing is impossible, Edna. Any objective can be taken. All we have to do is find the right tactics. The army taught me that much."

He turned his attention back to the map. The barn and corrals behind the building were made of stone and adobe; the only wooden structure on the place was a crude outhouse made of thin pine lumber. Setting fire to the main building was out of the question. Even if the timber and sod roof of the house would burn, there was always the chance the gunmen would leave Victoria inside to face an agonizing death.

Slocum leaned back in his chair, fired a cigarillo, and puffed a smoke ring toward the ceiling. "What do you make of it, Link? Any ideas?"

The young man stared at the map, brows bunched in concentration. "We can't go straight in," he said without looking up. "Somehow, we've got to catch them split up and take care of them one or two at a time, without the others knowing for sure what's happening."

Slocum squinted through the blue-gray haze of cigar smoke. "That's my thinking, Link. Divide the enemy and pick his forces apart. Exploit his weaknesses and neutralize his strength." The glimmer of a plan flickered into life in Slocum's brain. He reached for a bottle on the floor by his feet, twisted the top off, and poured a couple of ounces of whiskey into each of three water glasses.

He became aware that Link was staring at him. "You've got something in mind, Slocum." It wasn't a question.

Slocum nodded. "It's chancy at best. And, Link, I hate to say it, but the whole thing depends on how long they'll keep Victoria alive." He bent over the map, sipped at the whiskey, then leaned back in his chair. "Edna, we may need your help. You've already done more than your share and I don't want to see you in danger, but—"

"Slocum," Edna Dellafield interrupted, "I'm riding on this one. That's the end of that discussion. Now, let's hear this plan of yours."

* * *

Later, Slocum lay at Edna's side and stared at the ceiling.

"Something bothering you, Slocum?"

"Yes. You brought a lot of information back from Helltown, Edna. I've been wondering how you managed to do that."

"Easy. I lured one of Whiteside's men from a saloon. The ugly one, Jeb Dawson. He tends to get kind of talkative around a woman, especially when he's well on the way to falling-down drunk. Likes to boast a bit, that one."

Slocum's spirits skidded. "Edna, you didn't—" He left the question unfinished.

Edna chuckled in the darkness. "No, Slocum. I didn't. I let him fondle me a bit, maybe, while I was pouring whiskey down him. He passed out before anything more serious than that happened." She ran a hand down his chest. "Would you have cared?"

He patted the back of her hand. "A hell of a lot."

She sighed in contented lassitude. "Thank you, sir. You'll never know how good that sounds. To have someone care. Despite my slutty behavior toward you, Slocum, I am not a loose woman. I have high standards in men. Shut up and get some sleep," Edna said. "We've got a lot of work ahead of us tomorrow."

10

Slocum rode in silence along Helltown Trail, his mind sifting through the elements of his plan, looking for holes in the strategy. He found none—except for the small problem of keeping everyone alive in that scorpion's nest a few miles up the road.

He let his gaze drift from its constant sweep of the country-side to glance at his two companions. Neither of them had spoken a half dozen words since they had ridden out of Presidio. Link's features were grim, his jaw set. *The kid's got reason enough to worry,* Slocum thought. *He's got more to lose than anyone else in this little expedition.*

Edna Dellafield rode relaxed and outwardly confident, but Slocum saw the tension in the deep hazel eyes. He knew Edna's concern was not for her own safety, or even Slocum's or Link's, but for the young girl held captive. She had enough common sense to know the plan was chancy at best. He didn't worry about her not handling her end of the job. She was as tough on the outside as she was gentle on the inside. She led a fourth horse, a lean, leggy buckskin under a light saddle built for fast riding, not heavy range work. The buckskin would be—with luck—Victoria's mount in the flight from Helltown.

All three riders wore linen dusters despite the already intense heat of the early afternoon sun. Slocum insisted on the dusters because at a distance all riders looked alike in the long, flowing garments. Sweat trickled from Edna's brow beneath the man's hat she wore jammed tightly on her head. The Presidio store owner had grumbled about being roused from bed before dawn, but his bad temper faded fast as Slocum counted out the silver coins for the needed supplies. His grumbles turned to chuckles when Slocum added a gold double eagle to the stack for the man's troubles.

Slocum was astride the sorrel, his Winchester in the saddle boot and the spare .44-40 Colt Peacemaker he normally carried in his bedroll tucked beneath his belt. A few seconds saved by not having to reload a weapon could mean the difference between seeing today's sundown or the quick darkness of eternity. Link straddled his black, the big Winchester rifle resting across the pommel of the saddle and the .45 Colt in its holster at his belt. Edna rode Slocum's spare mount. She carried the double-barreled twenty-bore shotgun in a makeshift sling over a shoulder. *We may not get this job done,* Slocum thought grimly, *but if we don't, it sure as hell won't be for lack of good horseflesh or firepower.* So far, he admitted, their luck had held. There was no traffic on the Helltown Trail today. That made it less likely they would be seen and an alarm spread.

Two hours later, Slocum pulled the snorting sorrel to a stop on the low rise overlooking Helltown and studied the outlaw community. If Edna had missed anything in her scout of the town yesterday, Slocum didn't see it.

Helltown Trail angled between the two low hills on the east and west, wandered through what passed as the town square, and angled off toward the interior of Mexico. The big house where Preacher's gang had holed up stood isolated from the other buildings on the northeast side of town. There were two horses, both saddled, in the corral behind the house.

The square was flanked on the west by residences, boarding-houses, and a hotel; on the south by a row of cantinas and whorehouses; and on the east by a public livery stable backed by a log corral. A small stand of stunted mesquite trees lay just north of the stable along a shallow, dry creek that wandered past the livery before twisting eastward. A stone-walled well stood in the center of the plaza. Between the square and Whiteside's stronghold were three buildings. One was a gunsmith's shop, one a saddle and harness store, and the third was a long combination saloon and gambling establishment.

Slocum had planned the raid for midafternoon. He knew the outlaw breed. He had hunted them often and ridden with them on rare occasions, too. By the time the sun was halfway down the western sky, most of the gunmen would already have gone through enough whiskey to blur the eye and slow the reflexes. And they had to get Victoria Tucker out of there before sundown. Before Preacher Whiteside put her on the auction block in the town square.

The plan was simple enough on the surface. Slocum and Link would slip into town afoot, create a diversion, and hope-fully get into the Whiteside place and get Victoria out before the gunmen got organized. Edna was to stay with the horses, out of sight beyond the low ridge on the west side of the trail, and wait. Her shotgun was a bit of insurance against any pursuit. Slocum would have felt more comfortable if she had a howitzer or Gatling gun. Simple plans tended to get complicated as hell sometimes.

Slocum dismounted and turned to the two riders a step behind him. "It's time to get on with it," he said. "Better check those weapons one last time."

He heard the metallic clicks as Edna and Link again made sure their guns were loaded and ready to fire. He did the same with his own revolvers and rifle. A thick-bladed hunting knife rested in its sheath at his belt. Satisfied with the state of their armament, he raised an eyebrow. "Any questions?"

Edna shook her head as she dropped a handful of shotgun shells into a shirt pocket.

"All set, Slocum," Link said. "Let's go."

Slocum noted with satisfaction that the amber eyes had gone hard and cold. He nodded toward the big-bore rifle in Link's hand. "Better leave the long gun, Link. This will be pistol work. A close-quarter fight."

Link frowned, but thrust the rifle back into its sheath. Edna gathered the reins, tied Slocum's and Link's mounts to a mesquite tree with slipknots, and remounted. She held the reins of the spare horse firmly in one hand. Slocum stepped to the side of her horse and put a hand on her thigh. "Watch yourself, Edna. If this thing blows up on us, get the hell out of here and don't stop spurring until you hit Presidio."

She smiled at him, still outwardly calm. "Don't worry about me, Slocum," she said. "Watch your own hide." She grinned and winked. "Don't get anything shot off that we're not finished with yet."

The lewd wink and comment drained the last of the tension from Slocum's muscles. He felt the relaxed, alert calm of the hunt settle over his body. He gestured to Link, then turned and strode toward the dry wash leading toward Helltown, his movements smooth and silent as a stalking panther. Link followed, but not as quietly. His boots crunched in the sand and occasionally a twig popped beneath his foot. Slocum didn't bother to scold the young man. Link was doing his best, and it took years to learn the intricacies of the stalk.

The two men edged along the wash at a crouch, Slocum alert for a shout of discovery or the sight of movement along the creek bed. He heard or saw nothing. The wash dipped slightly until they could stand erect and still not be seen from the streets of Helltown.

Slocum waved Link to a stop in the scant shelter of the low mesquite trees and stared toward the livery stable with its log corrals a few strides away. Better than a dozen horses stood hipshot, head-to-tail, switching flies in the corral. Slocum climbed from the wash, eased his way to the back of the corral, and pulled the heavy knife. Sweat streamed from beneath his hatband as he sliced through the tough dry rawhide thongs that held the corral poles in place. He lowered each pole carefully and silently to the ground. It was time and effort Slocum didn't mind spending; he couldn't stand the thought of a good horse being hurt without reason. Finally, he slipped the knife back into its sheath and stood aside.

A couple of horses snorted tentatively and eyed the downed corral poles, probably sensing freedom but not yet willing to make a run for the gap in the fence. Slocum kept close to the poles that remained standing, worked his way to the back gate of the stable, and glanced inside.

A Mexican hostler dozed against a main support beam of the barn, his sombrero brim nodding as he snored. Slocum ignored the man for the moment. Then he spotted what he had hoped to see—a stack of dried prairie hay as tall as a man's shoulder, piled against a back wall of the barn. The haystack would make a good, smoky fire. And in dry country like this, a fire was the best diversion available.

Slocum pulled his Colt, strode silently to the sleeping hostler and cracked the man alongside the temple with the butt of the pistol. The hostler fell without a sound. Slocum knelt at the downed man's side and put his fingers against the dirty brown neck. The pulse was still strong. Slocum grunted in satisfaction. He hadn't hit him too hard. The man was unarmed, and Slocum never had believed in taking a life that was no threat to him. He dragged the hostler to the front of the livery, found a spot where the man would be safe from fire and smoke, and propped him in a sitting position against a wall. A casual passerby would think the man was simply asleep or drunk.

Slocum made his way back to the pile of prairie hay, scratched a lucifer into life, and held it to the edge of the pile. A wisp of smoke and small tongues of flame quickly flared in the stack of brittle, dry fodder. Slocum hurried from the barn, retraced his earlier steps in a crouching run, and was at Link's side in the mesquite grove before the first horses snorted and bolted through the gap in the corral. A trickle of smoke wafted from the rear of the livery.

"Get ready to move, Link. It's going to look like the fires of hell in there pretty quick."

Moments later the first shout of alarm sounded from the plaza. "Fire! Fire at the stable!" someone yelled.

In a matter of seconds the door of the main saloon and gambling hall burst open. Townsmen and armed outlaws swarmed into the street, pointing and yelling, then ran toward the livery to battle the blaze.

Slocum touched Link on the shoulder and nodded toward the back of the saloon. The two men stood and strode casually toward the rear of the building. Slocum's gaze flicked about; he expected to hear a shout of alarm, see a finger pointed toward them at any moment. But in the excitement of the fire, they reached the back of the saloon undetected. "Better pull that Colt now, Link," Slocum said. "You're getting better, but it still takes you longer to draw than it does for grandpa to take a piss. Go in with a full hand—and if it comes to shooting, remember that where you put the slug means a hell of a lot more than how quick you get it there."

Slocum swept the tail of his duster back, freeing the butt of the Colt for a quick draw if needed, pushed the back door open, and stepped inside. Four men who weren't busy fighting the blaze stood at the front door, looking down the street toward the stable. Slocum recognized two of the men; one was the wiry little Mexican gunman Jesus Quintana, the other the broad-shouldered and powerful Buck Teague. The third man had an apron tied around his waist and a bar rag in one hand. The fourth was medium-sized and fair-skinned, with a pistol carried low on his right hip.

"The Mexican and the big man," Slocum whispered to Link. "Part of Preacher's bunch. We've got no choice but to start here or there'll be guns at our back all the way. You take the big man. I don't know the others, but watch out for them. We don't know whose side they're on." Slocum heard the faint four-note clicks as Link drew the hammer of his pistol to full cock.

"Quintana!" Slocum called.

The muttered conversations at the front door stopped at Slocum's challenge. The four men turned as one. Quintana stiffened at the sight of the two men. The wiry Mexican's eyes narrowed as he stared at Slocum. "I know you," he said in Spanish.

"Damn right you do, Jesus," Slocum answered in the outlaw's native tongue. "Tlaxcala. About three years ago. You shot a good horse out from under me. I put a hole in your shoulder for that. I was going for your gut, but I missed that time. I won't now."

The Mexican leaned forward, his weight on the balls of his feet, his hand on the pistol at his belt. "Slocum! You son of a whore!"

Slocum slapped his hand to the butt of the Peacemaker at the same time Quintana drew. The Mexican was fast. His pistol was clear of its holster before Slocum's first .44 slug hammered into his chest. Quintana staggered back, his pistol still rising. Slocum thumbed the hammer, waited a fraction of a heartbeat to steady his aim, and squeezed the trigger. The soft lead slammed into Quintana's forehead; a red mist seemed to hang in the air as the impact of the heavy slug knocked Quintana through the open door and into the street.

Slocum heard the blast of Link's .45 almost atop the sound of his own pistol shots. He swung toward Buck Teague in time to see the man thrown against the wall by the wallop of a big slug. Link coolly thumbed the hammer; he didn't fight the recoil, and he took the extra half second to steady his aim. His second shot took Teague squarely in the middle shirt button before the other man could raise his pistol. Teague's chest seemed to cave in as the slug exploded out his back and spattered blood on the wall.

Slocum saw the pistol in the sandy-haired man's fist swing into line, the hole in the muzzle pointed dead on his shirt pocket. Slocum threw himself to the side, rolled, and fired more by instinct than by aim from the floor. The .44 slug hit the gunman beneath the chin and tore away the far side of his skull. The outlaw's pistol discharged in his dying convulsion. Slocum grunted as a sharp pain stabbed through his left shoulder; his arm went numb for an instant. He ignored the pain as he saw the bartender reach beneath his apron, pull a stubby handgun, and swing the weapon toward Link. Slocum twisted and slapped a shot toward the bartender, but he knew the slug had missed. Before he could thumb the hammer again, Link's .45 bellowed. The bartender folded at the middle, pistol flying, and slumped to the floor.

"Link! You all right?" Slocum could hardly hear his own words through the ringing in his ears. The blast of gunshots in a closed room had a way of plugging up a man's ears for a spell. A dense haze of spent powder smoke choked the room.

"I'm okay," Link said. "You?"

"Never mind! Bar that front door, quick!"

Link sprinted for the door, kicked a dead man's foot aside, slammed the heavy wooden portal shut, and dropped a thick bar into brackets on either doorjamb. There was only one way into the building now—the back door. But, Slocum knew, that also meant there was only one way out. And the gunmen outside would figure that out soon enough.

Slocum glanced at his shoulder. The end of a jagged sliver of wood protruded from the muscle near the joint, apparently torn from the wood of the bar by the fair-skinned man's final bullet. He tugged at the sliver and winced. The splinter was deep and ragged, the pain sharp, but it was something he'd just have to live with for a while. There wasn't time now to cut it free. He pulled himself to his feet and reloaded as his left arm regained its feeling.

Link hurried to Slocum's side and glanced at the spot of blood on his shoulder. "You hit, Slocum?"

"Nothing serious." Over the yells and commotion from outside, Slocum heard a fist hammer on the front door of the saloon. "The door will hold them back for a while, Link," he said. "We've got something more important to worry about now." He clicked the loading gate of his Colt shut and strode to the back door for a quick glance at the Whiteside house across the wide, sandy street. "We've got to get in there somehow and get Victoria out. Before that crazy son of a bitch decides to kill her."

Victoria Tucker huddled in the corner, struggled against the ropes at her wrists and ankles, and stared in growing desperation at the backs of the two men at the front window of the adobe building.

Preacher Whiteside and Jeb Dawson stared toward the pall of smoke at the rear of the stable for a moment, then ducked instinctively as gunfire crackled in the building across the street.

"What the hell's going on?" Dawson asked.

"How should I know, Jeb?" Whiteside pulled his revolver. "I'm going to go take a look. Cover me if anybody shoots this way."

Dawson palmed his own pistol and stood beside the window. He nodded. Whiteside swung the door open and stepped outside.

Adobe fragments sprayed across Whiteside's head a split second before the flat crack of a handgun barked from the back door of the saloon. Whiteside yelped and dove for the cover of a pile of firewood just outside the door. Jeb Dawson caught a glimpse of the tall man who had fired the shot, slapped a couple of slugs toward the saloon, then yelled at Whiteside: "It's that green-eyed bastard from the bank, Preacher! The one that shot Lloyd and Jubal!"

Victoria's heart pounded against her ribs. *They did send someone,* she thought; *I've got to get loose, slip away before these men decide to kill me.* She tugged harder against her ropes, felt the skin slip on her wrists. But she had gained a half inch of slack. She relaxed her muscles, let the blood from her wrists slick the ropes. *Just another few seconds, please, God,* she prayed silently.

"Where are the others?" Whiteside's voice was faint but calm from outside.

"Jesus and Buck went to have a drink," Dawson called back. He fired another blind shot toward the saloon door. "Reckon you can forget about them now, Preacher. Lollar went to the outhouse. Don't know where Dirk's at."

Victoria put all her strength and will into pulling against the ropes. The blood-slicked bindings slipped over the joints of her thumbs; a second later her hands were free. She reached toward the bedroll at her side, praying that Jeb Dawson wouldn't look around for just another few seconds. Her fingers groped in the folds of the bedroll and closed on the cold metal of the little .22 pistol. She pulled it to her, clutched it against her chest, and bent over to conceal the weapon. She had only the vaguest idea how to use it; pull the thing called a hammer back first, then point it and pull the trigger. Her breath caught in her throat at Preacher's yell from outside:

"They were warned! Kill the girl! Do it now, Jeb!"

Jeb Fowler turned from the window to stare at Victoria. Stained, broken teeth flashed dim against the dark skin of his stubbled face. "Why, I'd be just plumb happy to do that," he muttered. The flat blast of Preacher Whiteside's pistol sounded outside, answered by the splat of slugs against wood and echoes of gunshots.

Dawson strode toward Victoria. He made no attempt to raise the pistol and fire. She kept her gaze locked on his eyes as he crossed the room and stood before her. "Well, bitch," he said, "I reckon they'll keep old Preacher busy out there long enough for you and me to play some, first." He flicked a knife from his belt with his free hand and sliced the bonds from her feet. He unbuckled his gun belt and reached for the buttons of his pants. "Then, you little slut, I'll jam this pistol up to the cylinder in that sloppy pussy and pull the trigger. Just like I promised you I would."

Victoria still sat folded at the waist, her neck muscles strained from looking up at Jeb. He opened the last button of his trousers and let them fall around his ankles. He reached for her.

Victoria waited until she felt his hand grab the cloth of her shirt. Then she pulled back, thumbed the hammer of the pistol, jabbed it against his chest, and pulled the trigger.

The small pop of the little rimfire .22 cartridge was barely audible over the rattle of gunfire outside. Jeb Dawson's eyes widened in shock and surprise. He staggered back a half step. Victoria thumbed the hammer back, fired again—and again and again. Her heart sank in despair; she could see the puffs of dust from his shirt, the small smudges the little bullets left, and still he just stood there, looking at her in surprise. She kept firing until the hammer clicked on a spent cartridge. And still Jeb Dawson stood.

He started to lift the big pistol in his hand. The muzzle wavered, then shook, and the weapon seemed to drag his hand down. "Damn you—little bitch—" The pistol slipped from his fingers and dropped to the dirt floor. "You—shot me—" He sank to his knees, then toppled forward. The weight of his torso dropped across Victoria's legs, pinning her to the floor. She flailed at his head with the empty pistol; he grunted, but ignored the blows. He seemed to draw a deep breath. His hand crept toward the fallen pistol. It was just beyond his reach. Victoria tried frantically to yank her legs from beneath him. The weight was too much. And then sheer horror clamped a cold hand against her throat. Jeb Dawson's hand crabbed slowly toward the knife at his belt.

• • •

Link thumbed fresh loads into the .45, winced as a slug knocked adobe dust from the doorway, and glanced at Slocum. "One man on the roof of the house," Link said. "One inside, another behind the woodpile."

Slocum grunted. "The one on the roof's the half-breed. He's a hell of a good pistolero. That's Preacher behind the wood. Probably Dawson inside." He poked his head around the door, drew fire from the roof and front of the house, and ducked back inside. *Dammit,* Slocum thought bitterly, *we almost pulled it off. This is one godforsaken place to have to die in.* "They've got us pinned down same as we have them, Link." He sighed. "We're boxed in. I thought I had it figured, but it looks like I'm just going to get us all killed."

Link snapped a quick shot toward the woodpile. The sound of the lead on impact told Slocum nothing had been hit but kindling. Link drew back and glanced at Slocum. "I'm going after her," he said.

"Link, no! You'd just get yourself killed out there."

Link leveled a calm gaze on Slocum. "What the hell's the difference if I get killed out there or in here? At least this way Victoria has a chance. Can you cover me?"

Slocum saw the cold light of determination in the amber eyes. He pulled his second Peacemaker from his belt, ignored the twinge of pain in his shoulder, and nodded. "Like a damn blanket, son." He sighed. "Any time you're ready—" Slocum didn't have a chance to finish the statement.

Link bolted through the door. A rifle slug cracked the air by his ear as he ran, darting first to one side and then the other; a bullet kicked dust at his heels, another tugged at the flapping skirts of the duster. The firing slowed as Slocum hammered shots alternately toward the roof of the house and the woodpile, keeping the shooters pinned behind cover. Link heard Slocum's shouted warning above the roar of gunfire. He glanced toward the outhouse beyond the adobe, saw a man raise a pistol, and threw himself to the ground as smoke billowed from the gun. Link rolled, came to his knees, and squeezed a quick shot toward the man. He knew by instinct the slug went wild, but the gunman suddenly staggered back and fell. Slocum had nailed him.

Link sprang to his feet and sprinted the last few feet to the rough adobe wall. The overhang of the roof gave him some protection from the gunman overhead, and he was out of view of the man at the woodpile. He glanced into an open window. In the far corner of the room Victoria lay, her legs beneath a stocky man's shoulders. The man held a knife, its tip creeping toward Victoria's throat.

Link braced the .45 against the window frame, forced back his panic long enough to take a steady aim, and squeezed the trigger. For an instant he couldn't see through the powder smoke. Then the scene cleared. He saw the blocky man's body lying on its side. Half his head had been blown away.

Link clambered through the window and sprinted to Victoria's side. She was spattered with blood, her face ash white, eyes wide in fear and shock. "Victoria, it's Link." He reached out and shook her shoulder until the dazed expression began to fade from her eyes. "Are you all right?"

She nodded and mumbled something Link couldn't make out. "Can you stand up, Victoria? Can you run? We've got to get out of here!"

"I—think so. My feet have—been tied up so long—"

He helped her stand, felt her shudder, and then she all but collapsed against him. Link allowed himself a moment to simply hold her, feel the warmth of her body against his. He suddenly realized it was the first time Victoria had allowed him to touch her.

A sudden rustle from the roof above jarred Link back to reality. They were still trapped as long as that gunman was on the roof. He gently pushed Victoria aside, waited for the next whisper of sound from above, and triggered two quick shots toward the noise. He heard a surprised yelp over the blast of the gun, the scurry of boots retreating from above. *At least now he'll have something else to worry about,* Link thought as he ejected the spent cartridges and reloaded.

"We've got to make a run for it, Victoria," he said, somewhat surprised at the calm tone of his own voice. "We have horses on the ridge outside town. If we can make it that far, we've got a chance. Is there a back way out of here?"

Victoria tilted her head toward a doorway. "Back there, through that room. There's a window." She seemed to be regaining her composure, Link thought.

"All right, let's go," he said. "We'll just have to take a gamble that Slocum can keep that man on the roof occupied." Gunfire sounded from the street outside. Link knew that the outlaws were closing in on the saloon. On Slocum. *Maybe there's a way yet,* he thought, *if we can just get out of here alive.* He led Victoria to the back room and glanced out the window. *Nearly three hundred yards of open ground and half the gunfighters in Mexico looking for a target. Link, you dumb little bastard, you've always been too much of an optimist.*

He felt the first real push of fear against his bladder. Not fear for himself, but for Victoria. He listened for a moment to the gunfire outside. There was a brief lull in the shooting from inside the saloon. Slocum would be reloading, Link reasoned. He waited until he heard Slocum fire again, then practically pushed Victoria through the window.

"Run, Victoria!" he yelled as he swung down behind her. "Run for your life!"

A bullet hummed past Link's ear before they had covered four steps. Victoria stumbled; Link felt his heart skid in fear that she had been hit. Then she regained her footing. Her stride lengthened as blood pumped back into legs bound for too long. Link whirled and fired two quick, unaimed shots toward the roof, knowing his chances of a hit were poor, but hoping to buy time. Every stride they made was a step closer to safety.

A slug kicked dirt at his heels, another hit a rock at his side and screamed away into the distance. Link tried to keep his body between Victoria and the man on the roof, braced himself for the slam of a bullet into his back. *Just a few more yards and we'll be out of handgun range.* Even as the thought flashed through his brain, Link's gut knotted in despair and the thin hope faded.

Three men had managed to catch loose horses; now they charged in from Link's right, barely two hundred yards away and closing fast, rifles and pistols drawn. Link knew the horsemen would cut them down in seconds out here in the open.

A shallow depression edged by bear grass and prickly pear a few yards ahead caught his eye. He grabbed Victoria's arm, steered her to the depression, and pushed her down. He lay beside her, gasping for air, and leveled his Colt toward the approaching riders. He would wait until they came into sure handgun range. *We may go down here, damn your souls,* he thought, *but a couple of you are going with us.*

The horsemen, yelling and whooping, closed to within a hundred yards. Seventy-five yards. Link's finger tightened on the trigger. Then he blinked in disbelief as one of the horses stumbled, went down, and rolled over its rider. A split second later he heard the familiar, heavy blast of a big-bore rifle. He glanced toward the ridge, saw the puff of powder smoke there, and his spirits lifted. Edna Dellafield had grabbed Link's rifle and was firing toward the horsemen. Link heard the solid whop of lead against flesh; a heavy slug slammed a second man from his horse. The third reined in, confused, less than twenty yards away. Link shot him through the chest. The man slumped, then tumbled from the saddle. The reins had wrapped around his wrist; the horse snorted and danced nervously, trying to pull free. Link heaved himself from the shallow pit, sprinted to the horse, and grabbed the reins. He spent a precious couple of seconds untangling the reins from the dead man's wrist, then swung aboard the horse. He kneed the spooked mount toward Victoria, leaned down, grabbed her arm, and heaved her up behind the saddle. Then he yanked the reins and drove spurs into the horse in a wild charge toward the ridge. "We're going to make it, Victoria," he yelled over his shoulder. "We're going to make it!"

Slocum sagged against the wall beside the saloon door, thumbed fresh loads into his handgun, and watched as Link and Victoria disappeared behind the sheltering ridge. The cylinder of Slocum's Colt was almost too hot to touch. He flipped the loading gate shut.

A movement in the woodpile caught his attention. He raised the Peacemaker and waited patiently. Slugs chipped at the thick adobe walls of the saloon and the heavy thud of a battering ram sounded against the front door. *Haven't got much longer,*

Slocum thought, *but, by God, a bunch of these sons of bitches are running out of time, too.* The movement in the woodpile flickered again. A bit of cloth showed through a small opening in the logs. Slocum aimed carefully and stroked the trigger. Over the muzzle blast of the Colt he heard the satisfying whack of lead against flesh and Preacher Whiteside's scream.

"Dirk, help me! I'm hit!" Whiteside's thin cry sounded from the woodpile. Slocum snapped a quick shot to keep Whiteside's head down, looked toward the roof, and swore. He saw no movement atop the house, but the lowering sun showed the shadow of a man leaping from the roof to the ground behind the building. Slocum knew what the man was after—the two horses in the stone and adobe corral.

Slocum breathed a silent curse at the sound of wood splintering behind him. He dove behind the cover of the bar as the thick hardwood door began to buckle. The front door would go at any second. Slocum glanced along the bar and saw the saloon keeper's sawed-off double-barreled shotgun on a shelf. He holstered his Colt, scooped up the smoothbore, and swung the stubby barrels toward the front door. He cocked the heavy scrolled hammers.

The door splintered and burst open. "Come in, boys," Slocum yelled. He touched off both barrels. Two men in front went down as the cloud of buckshot ripped flesh; two others behind them yelped and dove for cover. Slocum placed the smoothbore on the bar. The shotgun had served its purpose for the moment; the men outside would think twice before charging that front door again.

Slocum heard the thud of hooves from the street behind the saloon. He yanked the Peacemaker from the holster and sprinted to the back door. Two men spurred mounts toward the edge of town. Preacher Whiteside slumped over the saddle horn, the tall half-breed at his side. Slocum aimed and squeezed. The slug thumped home in Whiteside's back, but the impact of the lead sounded strange to Slocum's ears. Then he realized his shot had hammered into the saddlebag draped over Whiteside's shoulder. The two men disappeared from view.

Slocum ducked aside as a slug thumped into the adobe near the back doorway. Two more random shots sounded, then a lull in the firing fell over the place called Helltown. Slocum knew it wouldn't last. The gunmen outside would be arguing over what to do now. With Whiteside gone, the men were without a firm leader. It would take them time to come up with a plan of attack. Slocum knew they would come after him. Helltown was full of tough, fearless men who would be thoroughly pissed off at a couple of strangers shooting up their town. At least Victoria and Link were safe. He mentally tipped his hat to the young Easterner. "Well, Link," he muttered aloud, "you and Edna pulled it off after all. Just be sure to make that banker pay you the money he owed me."

Slocum ran a hand along the cartridge belt at his waist. Only two rounds remained in the leather loops. Counting the loads in the two Colts, he had exactly thirteen cartridges left. He glanced around, took advantage of the lull in the firing to search the saloon's backbar shelves. In the compartment where the shotgun had been he found a cardboard box. He tore it open. There were six shot shells inside. He retrieved the sawed-off smoothbore, reloaded, and dropped the remaining four shells in a shirt pocket. *All right, boys,* he thought, *if you're going to come after me, let's get on with it. This is as good a place to die as any. Let's see how long you are on guts.*

He heard the scuffle of feet in the dust in back of the saloon, the mutter of voices from near the front door. They were going to rush him from both directions. Slocum cocked the smoothbore and waited.

The sound of lead against flesh and the sharp cry from just outside the door caught Slocum by surprise. Then he heard the heavy report of a big-bore rifle thunder along the street. The lighter, sharper whipcrack of Slocum's own .44-40 Winchester sounded; he heard the quick, frantic scuffle of boots away from the back wall of the saloon. The big-bore rifle fire continued, the shots evenly spaced. Aimed shots, not random noise.

"Slocum!"

He heard the distant cry over the thud of horses' hooves, glanced through the doorway, and felt his skin crawl. Edna Dellafield leaned low over the neck of her horse, leading Slocum's sorrel at a dead run down the back street of Helltown.

Slocum caught a glimpse of movement across the street from the corner of his vision, twisted, and saw a man lift a rifle toward the approaching rider. Slocum snapped the smoothbore barrels into line and pulled both triggers. The buckshot charge picked the rifleman from his feet and slammed him to the dirt. Slocum reloaded and fired one barrel wildly back along the street. Then Edna yanked her horse to a stop outside the door.

Slocum tossed the shotgun aside, sprinted through the door, and vaulted into the saddle. Edna had already spun her horse about. "Don't take all day, Slocum! There might be somebody in this damn town who can shoot straight!" With the yell, Edna dug her heels into her horse's ribs.

Slocum pulled his revolver as he yanked the sorrel around, slapped two quick shots toward shadowy figures along the wall, then touched his spurs to the sorrel.

Rifle and pistol slugs buzzed past, hummed overhead or kicked dirt at the heels of the horses. Slocum twisted in the saddle and emptied his Colt, firing wildly, intending only to drive the shooters to cover. The firing from the town stopped after he and Edna had covered better than a hundred yards. Moments later Slocum heard the pound of hooves behind them. Six of the outlaws had mounted and taken up the chase.

Slocum let the sorrel have its head. He dropped the empty Colt into its holster. His Winchester rested in his saddle boot. He pulled the rifle. The outlaws were little more than a hundred yards behind when Slocum and Edna skidded their horses to a stop and dismounted. Slocum ducked behind a cluster of stones and cactus at the edge of the trail, Edna at his side, the twenty-bore shotgun in her hand. Across the way, Link knelt behind a clump of bear grass, rifle aimed toward the pursuers. Victoria knelt at his side, Link's .45 in her hand.

Link's big rifle boomed. One of the outlaws tumbled over the rump of his horse. Slocum lined the sights of the Winchester, squeezed the trigger, and a second man jerked erect in the saddle, then fell. Link's rifle shot took down a third before the remaining three horsemen closed to within twenty yards. Edna's shotgun bellowed almost in Slocum's ear. The shot charge knocked a fourth rider from the saddle. The remaining two men yanked their horses around in a desperate sprint from the ambush.

They made about twenty yards. Link's Winchester slug hammered one man from the saddle. A split second later Slocum's rifle cracked; the last of the pursuers twisted in the saddle, sagged over his horse's neck, and after another ten yards tumbled into the dirt.

The raid on Helltown was over, Slocum thought; the outlaws wouldn't chance such losses again. And they were safe. He grinned at Edna. Her face was smeared with dirt, her auburn hair impossibly tangled, but she was the most beautiful thing Slocum had ever seen.

"Woman," he said, "if you ever pull a dumb stunt like that again, I'll turn you across my knee. You could have got yourself killed out there."

She grinned back at him. "There was something down there I wanted. I went and got it. And if you want to turn me across something, mister, I've got a suggestion."

Slocum chuckled aloud. He stood and led his horse across the road to where Link and Victoria stood side by side. Link was thumbing fresh cartridges into the loading port of the big-bore Winchester.

"Link, that was some damn fine rifle shooting," Slocum said. "And you didn't do half bad with the short gun down there, friend. I never expected to see any of you again."

Link flashed a weak smile in reply. "Couldn't leave you down there, Slocum. I'm not sure I know the way back to Kansas."

Slocum turned to the girl. Victoria's face was pale beneath the dirt and her hands trembled. "Are you all right, Miss Tucker?"

She nodded. "I'm not hurt." The last of the dazed look faded from her eyes. "Mr. Slocum, I'll never be able to repay you— and Link—for what you did. Those animals—"

"It's over, Victoria. You're safe now," Link said.

Slocum shifted his gaze toward the adobe settlement below. He had no idea how many men lay dead or wounded in Helltown. But there were still two unaccounted for. "Whiteside and the half-breed are out there somewhere, Link," he said. "We'd best keep a sharp eye out."

"Slocum, you're hurt!" Edna's voice at his side reminded Slocum of the wood sliver in his shoulder. The memory set it to stinging; in the excitement of the fight in Helltown and here on the trail, he had forgotten about it. "I'll see what I can do," Edna said.

"Not yet, Edna," Slocum said. "It'll keep until we get to town. I'm kind of anxious to see Presidio again."

11

The sun was still an hour above the horizon when Slocum led his small troop down the main street of Presidio.

Slocum's muscles had begun to rebel from the long hours and exertion. The tense exhilaration of the fight in Helltown had faded. Now his body felt drained and tired, his senses less alert. The splinter in his shoulder didn't help. The pain had grown from a minor nuisance to a deep, steady throb. His shoulder had started to stiffen, and he could feel the heat of the skin around the sliver. The thing had to come out soon, Slocum knew. It would be a sorry end to dodge all that hot lead and then die of blood poisoning from a little chunk of wood.

Victoria Tucker was totally exhausted. She nodded in the saddle as she rode alongside Link. Slocum was mildly surprised that she had lasted this long. No one, man or woman, could go through an ordeal like she had and still have strength left in either body or will. *The first thing we've got to do,* Slocum thought, *is get that girl a good, long sleep. Then a bath, some new clothes, and in a couple of days she'll be as strong as ever.*

He glanced at the woman riding at his side. Edna Dellafield carried her head erect, shoulders square, her hazel eyes bright, her smile quick. If there was any exhaustion in her, it didn't show. Slocum raised his already high opinion of the auburn-haired woman another notch. She wasn't just another attractive face over nice curves. The woman was tough as a new army boot.

Slocum reined in and turned to Link. "I'm going to stop off at the general store and pick up a few supplies," he said. "Take the women to the hotel. I'll be along in a few minutes." At Link's nod, Slocum reined his horse toward the store a few yards away.

The interior of the establishment was moderately cool despite the lingering heat of a scorching day. Slocum walked to the long counter laden with stacks of everything from cloth to candy to tobacco. The clerk on duty was the same man Slocum had roused before dawn.

"You sure do your shopping early and late, friend," the clerk said with a smile. "Was just about to close up. What can I do for you?"

"Two boxes of forty-four-forty cartridges and a box of forty-fives to start with," Slocum said. "A quart of Old Overholt, a dozen of your best cigarillos, some denatured alcohol, and a roll of bandages."

The clerk plopped the ammunition on the counter and studied Slocum's bloodstained shirt. "Not my call to be nosy, friend," he said, "but I've had a run on whiskey, ammunition, and bandages today. You get shot, too?"

Slocum's eyes narrowed, the pain in his shoulder forgotten. "What do you mean, 'too'?"

"Rider stopped by a half hour ago. Tall fellow, part Indian, most likely. Spooky eyes. Kind of a smoky color. Bought some medicine and bandages. Been a war somewhere I haven't heard about?"

"You might say that. This man—was he hit?"

The clerk shook his head. "Not as far as I could tell, but his friend was. I saw him through the window, sitting on his horse. There was blood on his shirt, down low on his side. Skinny cuss." The clerk finished filling Slocum's order and wrapped the goods in butcher paper. "That'll be four-fifty, friend."

Slocum pulled a ten-dollar gold piece from his pocket. "Any idea where those two might be?"

The clerk nodded, his gaze on the coin in Slocum's fingers. "Asked where they could get a room. I told them about Rosarita's. That's the whorehouse over on the east side. Doubt they'll get much rest, though. Rosie's place stays busy as all get out most every night. Noisy, too."

Slocum flipped the gold coin. The clerk caught it in midair. "Thanks. Keep the change," Slocum said. He picked up the bundle. "You're going to do some business again tomorrow morning," he said. "There'll be two ladies in here, needing clothes and other woman-type stuff. Give them whatever they need. We'll settle up later."

Slocum tucked the bundle under his left arm, winced as the movement stabbed the splinter deeper into his shoulder, and strode from the store. He stood for a moment, his gaze sweeping the street. *The war's not quite over yet,* he thought. *Presidio's in for a show tomorrow morning.*

An hour later, Slocum took a hefty swallow of whiskey and tried not to wince as Edna Dellafield finished digging the bloody splinter from his shoulder and doused the wound with alcohol.

"It doesn't look bad, Slocum," she said as she reached for a bandage. "A little inflamed, but I don't see any sign of blood poisoning." She dressed the wound and leaned over to kiss him on the cheek. "That better?"

Slocum cautiously flexed his left arm. The sting had already begun to fade; the muscles worked fine. "A lot better, Edna. Thanks."

Slocum reached instinctively for his Colt at the tap on the door. Edna beat him to it; Slocum's little .38 hideout gun seemed to appear in her fist from nowhere.

"Come in," Slocum called.

Link stepped into the room. "Hope I'm not interrupting something important," he said with a sly wink.

Edna grinned and lowered the .38. "If you had, I'd have shot you by now," she said. "How's Victoria?"

"Sound asleep." Relief and affection were plain in Link's tone. "She's worn down, and I think she might be in shock. When I told her she was going home, she just looked at me with this strange expression in her eyes and kind of shook her

head. But with rest, I think she'll be ready to travel in a day
or two." Link's gaze locked on Slocum's face. "When do we
go after those two, Slocum?"

"*We* don't," Slocum said emphatically. "I'm going, but I
want you to stay here with the women."

"Dammit, Slocum, I—"

"Don't argue with me, Link," Slocum interrupted. "That was
part of our deal."

Link's brow furrowed. "Look, Slocum, I know you're one
hell of a pistolero, but so are those two. I'd bet on you against
either one of them, but I'd switch the bet if you try them both.
It appears to me you could use some help."

Slocum shook his head firmly. "No, Link. I don't want
anything to happen to these women. Not after what they've
already been through. And in case you hadn't thought about
it yet, Victoria needs you. End of argument. I want your word
you'll stay out of it."

Link stared at Slocum for several heartbeats, his face flushed
in anger and disappointment. Then he sighed and shrugged.
"All right, Slocum. Get yourself killed if that's what you
want." The young man spun on a heel and stalked out the
door.

Edna was silent for several moments, staring toward the
door, then reached for the bottle and downed a stiff swallow.
"Slocum?"

"Yes?"

"Do you think maybe you made a mistake? I mean, going
up against two guns—" Her voice trailed away.

Slocum reached out and put his arm around her waist. "Maybe
be I did, Edna," he said, "but it was my call. I've got to lik-
ing that kid. He's not a gunfighter—not an eyeball-to-eyeball
shooter—and I'd hate like hell to see him get hurt."

Edna leaned her body against his. "And I suppose you think
I wouldn't hate like hell to see *you* get hurt?" She sighed. "I
didn't mind losing my husband, Slocum," she said, the worry
obvious in her tone, "but I don't want to lose you." She put
a finger on his lips to silence his objection. "I have no hold
on you, Slocum, and you have no hold on me. Either of us
can walk away at any time. But for now, you're all I've got.

And I'm growing used to having you around." She removed her finger from his lips.

"Edna, I—"

"Shut up, Slocum, and get undressed. I'm not finished with you yet." She leaned over and snuffed out the oil lamp.

Slocum leaned casually against the hitch rail of the café across the street from the place called Rosarita's, a cigarillo tucked in the corner of his mouth. He waited, let the relaxed calm loosen his muscles, and jiggled the Colt in its holster. The image of a small body broken by buckshot formed in his mind. Slocum held the sight this time, let it feed the icy knot of controlled rage in his chest. *It's payback time, Preacher,* he mentally promised the man in the house across the street.

He waited patiently as the sun rose. The street was almost deserted. Rosarita's had finally quieted down about four o'clock; Slocum had watched as the whores who worked the place left for their own beds, their night's work done. He tentatively flexed his left arm. The shoulder was a bit stiff and still hurt some, but it was of little concern. It wasn't his gun arm.

Slocum stared at the front door of Rosarita's and wondered idly if he had seen his last sunrise. He mentally shrugged the thought away. He knew it would come sometime, someplace, somewhere, and the knowledge didn't disturb him. He had come to grips with his own mortality during the war and had faced death many times since in frontier towns across the West. Today he sensed he might be pushing the odds. The half-breed had a reputation as a heller with a handgun, and Preacher Whiteside could handle a side arm almost as well. The odds weren't good, but he had faced worse.

Slocum's eyes narrowed as the door across the street opened and the two men he stalked stepped into the sunlight, the half-breed a stride ahead of the gangly Preacher. Slocum fought back the urge to do the sensible thing—pull the pistol and blow them both to hell before they knew what hit them. But that wouldn't do. Slocum wanted them to know why they died and who killed them.

He tossed the cigarillo away, his concentration fixed on the two men across the street, and started at the sound of footsteps at his left. He half turned, ready to draw and fire, then muttered a curse.

Link stood six feet away, his hand resting near the butt of his holstered Colt.

"Dammit, Link," Slocum growled, "you gave me your word you'd stay out of this."

Link never looked at Slocum. He kept his gaze locked on the two men approaching. "I lied," he said.

Slocum knew it was too late to argue now. Preacher Whiteside and Dirk Campbell were almost at the center of the street. Neither of the outlaws looked around them. They talked as they walked, unaware of the two men who had stepped from the boardwalk outside the café.

Slocum took two strides, closed the distance to less than twenty feet, then stopped, poised on the balls of his feet.

"Hello, Preacher," Slocum said.

The thin man started at the unexpected call. His lanky fame jarred erect. "You!" Rage replaced surprise in the weathered face. "You bastard! You ruined the whole plan!"

The half-breed's expression didn't change. Dirk Campbell stepped away from Preacher's side. His hand was already on the butt of the pistol in his gun belt. Slocum ignored the gunfighter. He planned to take Preacher first and hoped the half-breed would rush his shot and miss, or at least wouldn't hit anything vital.

"That's right, Preacher. I ruined it just like your men shot-gunned a woman to pieces in that Kansas bank. Now I'm going to kill you."

Whiteside's eyes narrowed; his right shoulder dipped as he clawed at the butt of the Colt. Slocum's palm slapped against the grips of his Peacemaker; his thumb hooked the hammer as the weapon started to slide from well-oiled leather. He flexed his knees to gain a crucial split second on the draw, eared the hammer to full cock as the weapon cleared the holster, his index finger lightly on the trigger. Whiteside's pistol came free; the weapon was partly raised when Slocum stroked the hair trigger of the .44-40. The slug walloped Whiteside high in the chest and jolted the thin man back a step. Whiteside's pistol barked, the slug tearing the earth harmlessly at his feet. At his side Slocum heard two gunshots, one almost atop the other, and the heavy whack of lead against flesh. Whiteside tried to steady himself and lift the pistol; Slocum took half a heartbeat to steady his aim and squeezed the trigger. The bridge of Whiteside's nose disappeared as his head snapped back. The shock of the slug's impact knocked Whiteside onto his back.

Slocum half spun, braced for an expected bullet shock, thumbed the hammer as his Colt reached the top of its recoil, ready to snap a quick shot at the gray-eyed gunman.

Slocum's eyes widened in surprise. The breed lay on his side in the dirt, boots twitching, blood spurting from a hole in his shirt pocket. Dirk Campbell's hand opened and the pistol toppled into the dirt. A dark stain spread at the breed's crotch as his bootheels kicked in death throes at the sand of the Presidio street.

Slocum turned to Link. The young man stood, his expression impassive as he stared at the gunman he had just killed. Slocum made no attempt to hide the surprise in his expression. A wisp of powder smoke trickled from the bore of Link's .45. The young man slowly lowered the pistol into its holster, then turned to Slocum.

"Still think I'm slower than grandpa's piss, Slocum?" Link asked. A faint grin touched the corner of his lips.

Slocum shook his head in disbelief. "Damn, Link. I had no idea you had gotten *that* fast."

Link's grin spread. "Maybe I'm as fast as you are now, Slocum. I hear a man slows down when he gets old."

Slocum's disbelief faded. He smiled back at Link. "You ungrateful, insubordinate, disrespectful young whelp," he said, "I ought to punch you one for that."

"Any time you're ready, old-timer," Link said with a chuckle. "But first things first. Didn't you say Whiteside was carrying a saddlebag when you shot at him back in Helltown?"

Slocum nodded.

"He's not carrying it now. Think we should check his room before the whores get to the money first?"

Slocum holstered his Colt and clapped Link on the shoulder. "By God, son, you're even starting to think. Let's go."

A sizable crowd had gathered around the bodies when Slocum and Link emerged from the brothel. Slocum had a set of saddlebags thrown over his right shoulder. It was heavier than he had expected.

Slocum glanced toward a short, stocky man kneeling beside the bodies. The man wore a star pinned to his vest. Slocum tapped a finger against the bullet hole he had put in one saddlebag and heard the clink of silver inside. "Wonder if bail money's a legitimate expense?"

Slocum stretched and yawned, then turned to the woman beside him. The window behind the hotel room curtain was still dark, but Slocum sensed dawn was near. It would be time to start home soon.

It was working out rather well, Slocum mused. The local law wasn't exactly heartbroken that Preacher Whiteside and the half-breed called Dirk Campbell were dead. Any tiny flicker of remorse winked out when the marshal heard the details of the robbery, murder, abduction, and shoot-out up in Kansas. He didn't even seem overly concerned that a goodly part of the population of Helltown had met a chunk of lead or two. A rather understanding man, Slocum thought.

And the heavy saddlebags still contained more than two thousand dollars, even after the two women were outfitted in new clothes and other female truck. Slocum knew it wasn't all bank money. Mrs. Tucker had told him the Scott's Ford bank never kept more than a thousand or so in ready cash. The rest stayed locked in her husband's safe until it was needed. Slocum would let the money counters haggle over what would happen to the leftovers after he collected his fee, his horse money, and a few dollars he had coming for expenses. He had tapped the banker's expense account for a costly new silk suit, some custom-made boots, and fresh trail clothes. A bonus of sorts as Slocum saw it.

He nudged a gentle elbow into Edna Dellafield's ribs. She came awake slowly—and snuggly. Slocum was feeling a little snuggly himself when the rap on the door sounded. Slocum reached for his Colt, more out of habit than anything else, checked to see that Edna was "decent," as she put it, and then called for the visitor to come in.

Link stepped into the room. His face was pale, brows wrinkled. Slocum thought he saw the faintest hint of moisture in the amber eyes. He also saw pain there, and hurt. A deep hurt.

"What is it, Link? Something wrong?"

"It's Victoria. She won't go home."

"What? Why—"

"Ask her yourself, Slocum. I've heard the story once. I'm not anxious to hear it again." Link spun on a heel and left. Slocum heard his retreating footsteps turn away from Victoria's room.

Slocum dressed quickly, but Edna was ready before he was. "I'm going with you, Slocum. Victoria may need a woman to talk to."

The two found Victoria fully dressed, seated in a chair at the window of her room. She had been crying.

"Victoria," Slocum said softly, "Link tells us you don't want to go home. Is that true?"

She nodded and wiped a hand across a tear-streaked cheek.

"Tell me why."

The tears started again when Victoria looked up at Slocum. "Because I can't face it—can't face him—again, Mr. Slocum."

Slocum's brows lifted in confusion. "Face who?"

"My father." The sudden bitterness in Victoria's voice startled Slocum.

"Victoria, I don't understand," Slocum said. "He wants you home enough to pay me to find you and bring you back—"

"So he can keep using me, dammit!" Victoria's voice cracked in rage and hurt. "Mr. Slocum, my father has been using me like—like a wife or a common whore since my twelfth birthday!"

"My God, Victoria," Edna said softly. Slocum heard the flare of outrage in Edna's voice. "You mean he—"

"I mean he came to my room almost every night, late, after Mother had gone to sleep." Victoria's tone had gone flat, almost emotionless, as if she were telling a story about someone else. "At first he just talked, about how I was growing up and all.

Then he made me use my hand on—on him. He rubbed my breasts and put his fingers between my legs. He said it was how little girls showed how much they love their fathers, and it was how fathers showed they loved their daughters."

Victoria lowered her gaze in humiliation. Tears dripped onto the cloth of her split riding skirt. "Not long after that he came one night and said it was time for me to really show him how much I loved him. He pushed my legs apart, and he put it between them and it hurt and—" Victoria's voice faded.

"Oh, dear God." Edna knelt beside Victoria, pulled her to her breast, and rocked back and forth, gently, as if trying to sooth a small child.

"He made me promise not—to tell Mother," Victoria said with a hiccuping sob. "He said it was our secret. That if I told the secret he'd—punish me. Then later, I couldn't bring myself to tell Mother. Even if she believed me, it would hurt her so."

Slocum sat for a moment, stunned at the girl's story. Then he felt the cold rage begin to build in his gut. "The son of a bitch," he muttered softly. "His own daughter. How could a man do that—" His voice trailed off as the fury grew.

Edna looked up at Slocum, the girl's head cradled to her breast. "It might be best if you left us alone, Slocum," she said. "Let me talk to her. Maybe I can help."

Slocum nodded. "There's someone else who might need a friend right now, too," he said. "I've got to go find Link before he does something dumb."

Slocum left the room, trying desperately to control the raw rage that boiled in his gut. *That dirty, sanctimonious son of a bitch; I'll kill the bastard myself, and I'll laugh while I do it—*

He managed to bring his need for blood under control by the time he found Link. The young man sat hunkered beside the stable, squatting on his heels, staring toward the horizon. The sunlight glistened on the tears on his cheeks. Slocum didn't hold that against him. There were times any man needed to cry.

"Link."

There was no answer.

Slocum squatted beside him, silent for a moment. He felt the sweat bead on his forehead and neck in the sultry heat. "It wasn't her fault," he finally said.

Link still stared into the distance. "I know that, Slocum. But, Christ, I could handle it better if she'd been raped by that gang of outlaws." The young man shuddered in revulsion and disgust. "Dammit, Slocum! Do you realize what that bastard did to his own daughter? I'll kill the son of a bitch for that."

"You may have to stand in line to do that, Link, and I'm in front of you." He put a fatherly hand on Link's shoulder. "I'm going to ask you something tough, Link, and I want a straight answer. No matter how much it hurts."

Link finally turned to look at Slocum. The pain and despair ran deep in the strange amber eyes. "Go ahead. Ask."

"Do you really love this girl?"

"Yes."

"Enough to help her handle this? Enough to help her put the past behind her as best she can? Enough to give her a new start in life?"

Link stared straight into Slocum's eyes. "Yes."

"She can't do it without you, son. I'd suggest a fresh start in a different part of the country. Ask her if she can understand that maybe one day she can feel a man's touch in the night without cringing. Then help her get to that point, Link. It's going to hurt, and it's going to be hard. A damn sight harder than facing a fast gun." Slocum squeezed Link's shoulder, then let his hand drop away. "I think you're enough of a man to handle that, if anyone can. I believe the girl loves you, but she just can't quite cope with the idea yet. Give it some thought. You two can leave anytime you want, to anyplace you want, if that's what you decide."

Link was silent for a moment, still staring into the distance. Then he sighed heavily. "I'll ask. If she still wants my help— if she even thinks she wants me—I'll do anything to help her." He finally glanced up. "Slocum, what are you going to do? About the money, I mean. There's quite a bit in those saddlebags. If I were you, I'd think long and hard about taking it and quitting the country."

Slocum reached for a cigarillo. "No, you wouldn't, Link.

You and I are more alike than you think. We're both saddled with a dumb concept called honor. It'll maybe get me killed some day." He scratched a match and lit the smoke. He had to admit the temptation was strong to take the money and run, but he knew he couldn't. "I made a deal. I may be a lot of things, but I don't break my word. I'll take it back to Kansas."

Slocum puffed out the match, squeezed the burned end between his fingers, and broke the stick. "That's more hard cash than I've ever seen at one time in my life, Link, but there are more important things in life than money. Sometimes a man like me needs to be reminded of that." He sighed wistfully and stood. "I'll be at the hotel. Let me know what you decide. All I ask is that you don't hurt the girl more than she's already been hurt."

Slocum was pacing the floor, trying to work off the disgust and anger that still boiled in his gut when Edna came back into the room four hours later.

"How is she?"

Edna flashed a wan smile. "She'll be all right now, Slocum. I think she has the strength to handle it. She's willing to go home now, at least for a day or two. We had a long talk. I convinced her that the first step in getting over everything that's happened to her is to confront her father. Face to face. Once she's done that, I think she'll be on the way back, with help. And she's getting some of that help now. Link's with her. They're preparing to leave for Kansas."

Slocum felt a surge of relief through his anger. Then another thought struck him, one that he knew he had been hiding from until this moment. "And you, Edna? What will you do?"

She looked deep into his eyes. "Slocum, I have no family, no friends, no money, and it's too damned hot in Presidio. I'd like to go with you to Kansas, if you'll let me tag along."

He held out his arms to her. "Edna," he said, "there is nothing I'd like better."

Slocum stood off to one side in the bank office in Scott's Ford, Kansas, battling the urge to pull his Colt and put a slug into the head of the man behind the desk.

The trip from Presidio had done little to soothe his smoldering hate for Will Tucker. The killing rage never quite subsided. Slocum's gut churned every time he looked into the man's eyes. Tucker had done the one thing Slocum could never comprehend, let alone tolerate or forgive. But the long ride home had served the others well. Link had been at Victoria's side the entire trip, at times talking quietly and often riding in silence, just being there for her. Edna Dellafield had spent many long hours at the campfire talking with the girl. Slocum spoke with Victoria frequently, but never about her experience. He hadn't the foggiest idea what he could say. This wasn't his kind of fight.

As the miles passed, Slocum had seen the slow emergence of Victoria Tucker from the wreckage of her inner pain. Now she stood, back straight, voice firm, head held high in defiance, before the man who had almost ruined her life.

Tucker sat with his head in his hands, a beaten man. At first he had tried to deny Victoria's charge, then to shift the blame to her. Nobody in the room bought either story. Finally, Tucker had caved in before the truth. He promised never to touch Victoria again, begged her to stay, apologized profusely and repeatedly to his wife. With this group, nothing he could do or say would help, and Tucker now realized that fact. *The bastard knows he's about a half inch from a noose or a slug,* Slocum grumbled inwardly, *and all the whining in the world won't change that.*

Mrs. Tucker stood at the side of the desk, her back ramrod straight, glaring in disgust and rage at her husband. Tucker looked up at her, tears in his eyes.

"Margaret, I—"

"Shut up, you sniveling bastard," his wife said, ice in her voice. "I'm damned close to killing you where you sit."

"I'll loan you my pistol," Slocum cut in, his voice as cold as the woman's, "or I'll pull the trigger on him myself, if you want. It would be my pleasure."

Margaret Tucker glanced at Slocum. "He isn't worth the price of a cartridge, Mr. Slocum. I will take care of this pile of dog droppings in my own fashion. If Mr. Tucker here is lucky, he will escape with his balls—but with damn little else."

Slocum almost grinned despite the disgust that churned his

gut. Will Tucker might be one sorry son of a bitch, Slocum mused, but his wife was a hell of a woman. He glanced toward Victoria, standing beside Link. The young couple stood with jawlines firm, dry-eyed, facing the first difficult step together. Slocum decided he liked the sight.

Margaret Tucker turned to face the group. "If you ladies and gentlemen will excuse me for a while, I have some business to attend to with Mr. Tucker. I would like to ask you all to come to my house tonight after dinner. We have many things to discuss."

Slocum saw Link slip his hand beneath Victoria's elbow and gently lead her toward the door. Edna followed, a step behind. Slocum tipped his hat to Mrs. Tucker in a silent salute and followed the others. *By the time that woman is through with him,* Slocum thought with a measure of satisfaction as he strode from the bank, *Will Tucker may wish I'd shot him in the head after all.*

Slocum, clad in his new expense-money silk suit, escorted Edna Dellafield into the parlor of the Tucker home. Margaret Tucker greeted them cordially. Link had already arrived.

"Mrs. Dellafield, would you loan me Mr. Slocum for a moment? We have a bit of unfinished business. Victoria will get you a drink if you wish. We have everything from fine imported French wine to the old skullbuster called Kansas sheep-dip by the cowboys hereabouts."

Edna smiled, nodded, and made her way into the main dining room. Slocum heard a girlish giggle from the room and realized with a start that it was the first time he had heard Victoria Tucker laugh aloud. It was a pleasant sound.

Margaret Tucker led Slocum into a small room which obviously served as a home office, poured him a double whiskey from a bottle of fine Tennessee sour mash, then dribbled a shot into a glass for herself. She waved toward a chair alongside a rolltop desk. "Have a seat, please," she said.

Slocum settled into the comfortably overstuffed chair and sipped at the whiskey. It was superb stuff, smooth and mellow. Margaret Tucker sat in the leather chair behind the desk and lifted her glass in a toast.

"Mr. Slocum, I cannot thank you enough for bringing Victoria home safely. Money is not sufficient, but perhaps it will help." She pushed a leather pouch toward him. "This is the money promised you as a reward, plus expenses, plus your own three hundred dollars taken in the robbery, and a bonus. You've earned every dime of it, Mr. Slocum, along with my everlasting gratitude."

She tipped the glass and downed the whiskey in a single swallow. "You may wish to count it," she said, her face coloring slightly, "considering that I seem to have made at least one terrible mistake in the last few years."

Slocum tucked the pouch into a pocket. "No need to count it, Mrs. Tucker. If you say it's all there, that's good enough for me."

A brief look of self-disgust flickered in Margaret Tucker's eyes. "I've been a fool, Mr. Slocum. I lived with that man for twenty years, and never really knew him. Or perhaps I did and simply refused to admit it. I understand a lot of things now that baffled me before. Especially the abrupt change in Victoria."

She fell silent for a moment, turning the whiskey glass in long, delicate fingers. Then she sighed and smiled. The change in her expression reminded Slocum of the grinding emotions she had gone through during the day. "Victoria and Link will be leaving for San Francisco within the week," she said. There was a sad note to her voice. "Link, it seems, is quite a wealthy young man in his own right. I expect him to do rather well on the West Coast. There are so many opportunities there for the young." The smile faded; Slocum thought the woman's eyes misted slightly. "I will miss Victoria greatly. I failed her as a mother and as a woman. That is my burden in this whole sordid business. But she will be in good hands." She inclined her head toward Slocum. "Link rode away from here a brash young boy. He came back a man. You taught him well, sir."

"Boys grow up in a hurry where he's been, Mrs. Tucker. Link's a good man," Slocum said softly. "If anyone can help your daughter get over this, he can."

"Being away from this house, this town, should help her forget," Margaret Tucker added. Then she shook her head. "That isn't correct. A girl can never forget something like that.

But at least she will have the opportunity to learn to cope with the past."

"And you, Mrs. Tucker. What will you do?"

She picked up the bottle and refilled both their glasses. "I have a bank to run."

Slocum raised an eyebrow. "Will your customers deal with a woman banker?"

"They'll get used to the idea," she said. "It was my inheritance that started the institution in the first place. I've stayed in the background, but I've been making the major decisions on investments and operations ever since the doors opened." She leaned back in her chair and smiled at Slocum. "I may seem on the surface to be an ordinary housewife who happens to have married into money, Mr. Slocum. The truth was quite the reverse. I'm a woman, but I've never considered myself a weakling. And I do have some talents other than sweeping and mopping floors."

Slocum returned her smile. "Somehow that doesn't surprise me a great deal, Mrs. Tucker." His smile faded abruptly. "What about your husband?"

Margaret Tucker leaned forward, her elbows resting on the desk. "Control of the bank was part of my agreement with Mr. Tucker. In exchange, he received one horse, one saddle, two hundred dollars in traveling money, and got to keep his prized testicles and his life—precisely what he brought into this marriage. He has departed with my earnest request that he never return to Kansas. Along with the threat of castration by rusty knife if he ever attempts to see or contact my daughter again."

Slocum nodded. It served the son of a bitch right, he mused. This woman knew more than one way to extract an eye for an eye.

"I've also made Edna an offer of employment," Mrs. Tucker said. "She's quite intelligent, well educated, and I will need help running the bank. She has agreed to be my assistant manager and chief cashier. I believe she will like it here in Scott's Ford. It's not a bad town except for a few dirty little secrets." She sipped at the glass. "What are your plans, Mr. Slocum? Scott's Ford could use a man like you. I do have some influence. You could begin as city marshal and move up to sheriff in the next election."

Slocum smiled and shook his head. "I've never been too keen on carrying a badge, Mrs. Tucker. They tend to draw lead. I may someday be shot dead by a drunk cowboy, but if that happens it will be a coincidence, not part of the job." He leaned back, sipped at the bourbon, and savored the warm glow it left in his stomach. "Besides, Mrs. Tucker, I have something of a reputation with a gun. That tends to draw trouble. A lot of men would like to boast they were the shooter who killed the man called Slocum. You don't need that kind of a drawing card here. As you say, it's a nice town."

Slocum turned to glance out the window. "I'll admit there are times when I think about settling down." He chuckled softly. "But by the time I have a couple of drinks and a good cigar, the urge goes away. I'll be moving on soon. There's a lot of country I haven't seen yet."

Margaret Tucker pushed back her chair and stood. "In many ways, Mr. Slocum, I envy you. I envy your freedom. And your courage. Frankly, sir, it takes one hell of a man to ride into a nest of outlaws the way you did."

Slocum rose and stared at the banker's wife in open admiration. "Mrs. Tucker, what you've done and what you're doing takes more guts than just pulling a trigger." He offered his arm. "I would be honored to escort you back to the gathering."

A full moon washed over the streets of Scott's Ford as Slocum and Edna Dellafield strode side by side from the Tucker home toward the hotel a couple of blocks away. Slocum's left arm was around Edna's waist, the warmth of her comforting against his hand.

"Slocum," Edna said, mischief in her tone, "Margaret won't be needing me at the bank until Monday, and this is only Friday." She patted him on the rump with her free hand. "Got any plans for the weekend, cowboy?"

Slocum grinned down at her. "We'll think of something," he said.

If you enjoyed this book, subscribe now and get...

TWO FREE

A $7.00 VALUE–

If you would like to read more of the very best, most exciting, adventurous, action-packed Westerns being published today, you'll want to subscribe to True Value's Western Home Subscription Service.

Each month the editors of True Value will select the 6 very best Westerns from America's leading publishers for special readers like you. You'll be able to preview these new titles as soon as they are published, *FREE* for ten days with no obligation!

TWO FREE BOOKS

When you subscribe, we'll send you your first month's shipment of the newest and best 6 Westerns for you to preview. With your first shipment, two of these books will be yours as our introductory gift to you absolutely *FREE* (a $7.00 value), regardless of what you decide to do. If you like them, as much as we think you will, keep all six books but pay for just 4 at the low subscriber rate of just $2.75 each. If you decide to return them, keep 2 of the titles as our gift. No obligation.

Special Subscriber Savings

When you become a True Value subscriber you'll save money several ways. First, all regular monthly selections will be billed at the low subscriber price of just $2.75 each. That's at least a savings of $4.50 each month below the publishers price. Second, there is never any shipping, handling or other hidden charges—*Free home delivery*. What's more there is no minimum number of books you must buy, you may return any selection for full credit and you can cancel your subscription at any time. A TRUE VALUE!